CANDLES AND DARK NIGHT

Candles and Dark Night

GRACE INGOLDBY

HEINEMANN : LONDON

This book was written with help
from The Society of Authors.

William Heinemann Ltd
Michelin House, 81 Fulham Road, London SW3 6RB
LONDON MELBOURNE AUCKLAND

First published 1992
Copyright © Grace Ingoldby 1992

The author has asserted her moral rights

A CIP catalogue record for this book
is held by the British Library
ISBN 0 434 36534 3

Phototypeset by Intype, London
Printed in Great Britain
by St. Edmundsbury Press, Bury St. Edmunds

One

I have never known love but as a kiss
In the mid-battle, and a difficult truce
Of oil and water, candles and dark night,
Hillside and hollow, the hot-footed sun
And the cold, sliding, slippery-footed moon –
A brief forgiveness between opposites
That have been hatreds for three times the age
Of this long-'stablished ground.

On Baile's Strand
W. B. YEATS

ONE

Up there they rip the trees apart to celebrate a wedding, something's got to give. They hack the yew and fir mechanically, branches crashing to the frozen ground. Twin boys, the Freres, are detailed to do the donkey work. Nine-year-olds, wrapped up well against the weather, they have no choice but to get on with it, more or less. One fools around the saw bench a bit but maintains a fairly wide arc round his father, the other, silent – not something you'd like to meet on a dark night – works in demented spurts.

Part of the morning and into afternoon they work at it, load themselves up with the green branches, trailing and breaking, catching and snagging them, laying them so that they overlap. So the steep path to the church is dressed, made artificially green in December, when all else up there is bleached and petrified, iron for inches down.

The sky is high and washed-out blue, the silence almost absolute, and somehow it seems that this sky, this silence, this cold that penetrates every living thing, has corroded the link between this place and any other. This is a hard place to be living in, this is a place miles above sea level: this is Carver Hill.

Freewheeling out of town, across the bridge, beyond the tannery, Dora on the journey up to Carver, cycling in a sort of ecstasy, thinking about sex. Swinging round the bends that edge the lake she wants to yell, 'Delivery!'

Wreaths in the hedges celebrate the dead, but she won't look at them; what on earth's the point? Dora's country has fought itself almost to a standstill, but still they won't give up. Bloody torsos lunging at one another, that's how she sees it, fighting men backed by fatuous women who fed them up for it, ironed their shirts. Hardened campaigners meeting in no-man's-land who call a halt for just a moment, catch their breath,

'I'm a bit deaf since the explosion and you have lost an eye, but prop ourselves up against a tree, why don't we, before I take your arm, you sever my leg?'

The wreaths in the hedges meant something but not everything. It was just possible there was more to life than this.

Stephen cycled in front of her. What did Stephen see? She could pretend she didn't guess. Guess that he saw bridges, highland, woodland cover, what was farmed now, what was left to waste. He saw, well they all did, old battles and future skirmishes. Woodland meant skirmishes, woodland, lying on a bed of dried bracken, meant sex.

They pushed up the big hills; after the lake it was uphill all the way, and the bikes hadn't a three-speed between them. She tried to hook his eye to hers when he turned back to encourage her but when he wasn't looking her young mouth lapsed a bit. Two for One, the posters read.

Cycling out from the town on the two great lakes and into the cold country, the country at a time of civil war. War, her impulse was to make slight of it, trite of it, she could teach a course on it, 'The war is not done so long as my enemy lives.' On the road like this one could see it in a new perspective. War was places on a map that strangers learn to pronounce properly, places triggering a memory, death at the crossroads or where the bus stopped.

'I'm going to live outside history,' Dora said. The wreath in the hedge, the writing on the road, she'd wheel her bike with expertise around them. Riding behind Stephen, she adored his back. How one worships the beloved, how his elbow means something, his ankle bone, the heel of an ordinary shoe. All his clothes were somebody else's, didn't quite fit; this morning it was two scarves around a hat.

Her mother spoke to her in her room, 'I want to speak to you,' speaking not being in the general run of things. 'I want to speak to you Dora.'

About sex?

'People who come from where Stephen comes from are dirt poor.'

A horrible expression, mean; her mother had left the ironing board, the chopping-block, the oven, to talk to Dora about poverty, a subject she knew precious little about. About poverty and its related diseases perhaps, for her mother set great store by cleanliness. About lice perhaps or impetigo, ringworm, TB, rickets? Hands clutching the apron, there is always more. Out comes the corner of a hanky, the twist of pastel tissue, whatever it is it's meant to make Dora prostrate herself in guilt.

Here it comes, prostrate yourself. 'Children from Midway and Carver used to wear mufflers under their jackets when they didn't have a shirt.'

Incontrovertible proof that Dora was heading in the wrong direction: two scarves round a hat!

Stephen was clean and beautiful. She'd known him as a child. He was different, from the country he'd passed into high school and come to lodge with Dora's parents in the town. Everything about him was lovely: he had beautiful writing, she remembered the notebooks he wrote in, his name on the cover in blue-black ink, and she would kiss his name. He could draw and he could copy, put a table mat of a bird or a flower in front of him and he'd draw that. He said that at his house one whole ceiling was a painting of heaven with angels on it and those who knew Stephen confirmed that it was true.

You felt guilty if you lied to Stephen though he could lie to you. He wouldn't make a fist of school, he didn't see the point. The teachers were particularly unsubtle: after the first few weeks of term, talk of Stephen centred on how he might be saved. How he could be lifted up and out of things and distanced from his background, helped. They cornered him; it seemed improbable to imagine now, but even her father had a go. Do things this way, that way, bigger better, at fourteen Stephen was too old to turn. 'My life is where I come from,' he would say or something like it. Dora was terribly impressed.

Dora remembered conversations he had probably forgotten. The little knock on her bedroom door that announced him, he'd come to talk to her, to Dora, and she was only eight. Talk. He wasn't the type for doctors and nurses, he didn't want to see your pants; this was and wasn't a relief. He didn't roll around and fight either, he wouldn't make a noose round your teddy's neck and hang him high where you couldn't reach him, he knocked before entering, came in on a mission to explain.

He used her dolls' house as an example, pipe-cleaner mice in human clothing bent to make his point. Their world was small but it had everything in it that anyone could ever need; the sun came up and the sun went down on them – you'd kill for that quiet voice. The implication was that his world – somewhat shadowy, very far away – was infinitely better than her world; she knew instinctively that this was not a matter for debate. Dolls' house talk was serious anyway, he was a pedant and he really didn't like it when she butted in.

The dolls' house table was wobbly, well he would put a leg on it: mend one table so it stands forever rather than tackling all the tables in the world. He said that or some equivalent, it didn't really matter what he said or what it meant in those days; he was in her room not her brother's, that meant a good deal. It didn't matter what he said, it was the way he handled objects, gently, with determination, the sound of what he said more than the sense of it.

'The people in this dolls' house get up and go to bed, they eat and sleep . . .'

'And play,' said Dora.

'They eat and sleep and play. They know who they are and they know where they came from . . .'

'They came from Bests actually . . .'

'They take it in with their mother's milk.'

She dared herself to repeat his words, 'Mother's milk.'

He was far less bouncy than other boys, and she had got him, living in her house! The very slowness of him appealed to her immensely. There was no urgency about Stephen, he wouldn't rush, he didn't see the point of getting on. The lull of his voice, his mild manners, everyone who met him was affected by him. He had imitators at school who aped the little things: the way he'd light a cigarette, another reason the teachers felt he was one to corner, one to get. Her brother, with whom he shared a room, hero-worshipped him, dogged his every step. Heaven, but it didn't last for long. Stephen gave up school, left the Parks's house on Mill Street after the winter term.

Stephen passed out of their lives, brother and sister grew closer after he had left. Mother cut out sewing on the table he had drawn on, other children came to lodge with them, laid their bodies on his bed. If now and then Dora heard news of him she still felt a little shiver of expectation, like the wind that gets up slightly before a shower of rain. The last she'd heard was that he had gone away in rather a hurry; her parents blamed the war of course, 'Caught up in something I shouldn't wonder.'

All that.

The fight went on without him, her brother joined it, no one did or said anything to stop him, what was there to say? Truancy was up at school, suicide kept low, balladeers and poets found a springboard to write from, emigration left the houses empty, snapping something vital in the soul. For those who chose to stay and keep their heads down, trouble was just something you got used to. Euphemism flourished, anecdote told the truth, in town on Mill Street life had a hysterical edge to it. Broken hearts were two a penny but boredom was unheard of; unwittingly they all became accustomed to, reliant on, the background noise.

'But you could at least wait until things calm down, Dora.'

Dora pursed her lips.

'Waiting never killed anyone.'

Dora knew it did.

Dora could tell you, graphically, about people she knew positively prostrated by waiting, prostrated was a favourite word. Her brother fell or was pushed, 'unlucky' was the word they used; they'd buried him last June. Since his death her father had remained vertical by a whisper, held up by his sock suspenders and the buttons on his collars and his cuffs. She liked to imagine her parents' bodies laid out, dissected on a slab, for death has dealt a body blow: internal organs all hunched up now, compressed, compacted, the heart just a pump. Even from the outside you could tell if you had an eye for it, the numbed cordiality of life on Mill Street, the long silences of awful mealtimes, mother with the pastel tissues, father who cried incontinently into the fur of a favourite cat. Delivery, Dora had to save herself, to strike out for the floating log, for people died inside from waiting or from shame or grief – from frustration even – Dora thought of sex.

The silence of the countryside, the silence of which people were justifiably scared stiff. The sound of bike wheels on the road surface, silence before and after, and in that silence little animals, stoats and weasels, held their breath. Oh dear and in that silence, deepened by the winter, a woman would simply ride behind her future husband and, forgetting everything else, now wish she wasn't desperate for the loo. A long journey ahead of her, the saddle made it considerably worse. When she hung back, he would wait for her until – she could have done without this – she had to make some explanation, call to him, had to stop and let him go ahead of her and around the corner, 'Don't wait Stephen. Go on. I'll catch you up.'

Almost lunchtime, they dropped down to a scattered village set along the road. Empty houses, roofs gone, gables standing, years of trouble and its sequel emigration. Stephen, who took an interest in all sorts of things that bored her, did she mind if he stopped for a moment?

She was keen to stop.

Stephen poking about a bit, bending to go through a doorway, empty houses, it probably wasn't safe. Listening in the silence to his scuffing boots, old newspapers, tin cans. They could have lunch here though of course she wasn't hungry, sit in the winter sunshine.

'We could make a fire?' They could gather wood from round about, make a fire and he would undress her and they could lie on the awful coat her mother had insisted on. Come on Stephen!

Was Stephen about to take out an exercise book,

draw the view? He poked about a bit and when they ate they ate on the roadside standing up. The grass after a hard frost was now soaking after an hour or so of sun, and where they stood, thought Dora, where they stood and ate would after they left remain indented for some time.

He wasn't at ease with her, he seemed preoccupied. He added to the silence on that road. She wasn't shy with him, she could speak; she couldn't tease him quite as she'd teased him the night before, but she could speak. She leant back in the sun against the wreck of the house she'd like to have made love in, making love with Stephen by a spitting fire. Stephen stroked the warm pale stone, spoke for a moment of where it would originally have been quarried, how in those days they would have brought it down and, as he talked, she thought of how he was becoming, more and more and rather terrifyingly, a bit of a stranger to her now. She thought of how she'd teased him yesterday, what had happened to the confidence she'd had then? He didn't even look at her, if only he would look at her. Was he protecting himself? He wouldn't catch her eye.

'Time is not elastic, Stephen,' she ought to warn him, 'time is very short.' If he would only take her hand or something, one small gesture. How obsessed she felt this morning, watching the hand that stroked the stone.

She learnt later that when Stephen chose his words with care he was lying; perhaps she knew already but pushed the knowing to one side. He'd told her that he had come home because his mother was dying, he'd come back to cope with that. She died in November and he had drifted on in the empty house. He hadn't been lonely, he liked the sound of his own footsteps – she liked the sound of his quiet voice.

He'd been away a long time, described his home-coming as a sort of winding down.

'I want you to feel that you're absolutely free,' he'd said when he proposed to her.

'I want you to feel,' she'd wanted to tell him, 'that you're absolutely caught.'

And events had conspired in their favour, a foreign peace-keeping force had since the summer pushed slowly westwards. If all accounts were to be believed, Dora and Stephen had re-met on the eve of lasting peace. Dora's brother wouldn't see it. What did it say on the gravestone? Something vacuous about the end of earthly trials, peace eternal? Her brother: killed in an ambush, in a scattered village just like this? Knowing where is important, knowing how and when, time of death, position of corpse, last words, 'Love to mother'? Her parents didn't know, they didn't want to talk about it. Her mother was disgusted, said she didn't have a son.

Stephen . . . Dora wondered. With Stephen, one fine day, in bed perhaps, or what is it that cosy married couples do? Talking after dinner by the fire? With Stephen, would she be able, when they really knew each other, to talk to him properly about her brother? Would she feel safe with Stephen, safe enough to talk about the underneath of things? To think aloud and not worry about making a fool of herself, to talk like the lyrics in popular songs, to give it to him straight from the bottom of her heart?

Would cosiness bring confidence, did marriage mean an end to isolation? Could she tell him about mourning for her brother, what it was like for her – death, not sex?

According to the priest, the knack of grieving was choosing to let go: pigs really might fly? One couldn't forget but it was sinful to indulge oneself in remembering the little things, going over and over it all. Her brother's hair when he first got up in the morning, how he had to damp it in front of the mirror to make the top lie flat. Remembering that was a sin. And guilt, 'Don't dwell on it, Dora.' What did those pious bastards know? Dora felt guilty, and Stephen should feel guilty too. It was partly to do with Stephen, it was Stephen's cause.

For a year and a half she had driven her brother to pick-up points, driven him out of town somewhere until they reached a place where it would be safer for her – 'Be sensible' – to turn back. Now it was time to kiss him goodbye, make a joke if she could rise to one, goodbye. Kissing. The kissing bit was great. You kissed your brother physically knowing that mentally your brother wasn't there. He corpsed on her and she could feel it in his fingers as he touched her, as she offered up her living cheek. Guilty of grieving, Dora leaning on her handlebars, waiting again for Stephen who was looking at the view.

Her brother came back to get his strength up, to pick up his clean shirts. Messages came to him and off he'd go again. A piece of paper with a name on it, a nod of the head in the market, something slipped into a folded newspaper, the hand on the shoulder at the bar, 'Turn to your left now, slowly, see there in the corner?'

He never said when he expected to go again. He didn't run his own life any more and the last time he'd gone she'd been so upset by him that she hadn't bothered with the condoning kiss.

Never, ever let anyone go from you without a touch, a kiss, a handshake, something, anything, proper words amounting to farewell; if she ever had any children she would teach them that.

'Say goodbye properly, Dora.'

'No.'

Christ. If there could just be a small torrential downpour; sheltering under a tree, her coat, the bracken . . . Her legs were tired now, her hands and face felt flat with cold, her nose was probably bright red. That high and washed-out winter sky, a cracking, crisp day in December. But mentally for Dora, as they rode on into the afternoon, a depression loomed. She thought less and less about sex and more and more of apprehension and nerves and about what gates were opening and what gates closing in her life, about what opening and closing gates meant.

In opposition to her marriage Dora's parents formed a double act. She brought the two of them together for once, the whole house became a stage. One cued the other, perfect timing, clear delivery, 'He'll have you out in some field picking up potatoes. Keeping house for a collection of miserable old peasants.'

'It'll make mincemeat of your hands.'

'Down in some dive or other in Midway, drinking spirits . . .'

'Like some sort of moll.'

They couldn't remember the mild boy who'd lodged with them and sometimes wet his bed. They blamed the war; now they didn't have a daughter or a son.

Only now did she begin to consider it coolly: life in a different household among strangers. Cycling alongside him – for he was at last more relaxed with her – pointing out familiar landmarks, well landmarks familiar to him, she became more yes and no and less, far less, the flirtatious, future bride of lunchtime.

She had thought only of the opening of the gates, of going, not of leaving house and home. Up here on the plateau, a positive sea of bleached old hills, trees here, sheep there, smoke from the cement works at Midway in the distance, pausing before the last push up. He pointed to a field barn on the horizon, the turn marked Carver, Gobbins, Starveall, turning up and away from Midway, up and into IT.

Wasn't the dull and dismal round at home preferable to the effort, the effort of the new? She didn't know Stephen or anyone else there and she felt a mounting panic, the effort of the new. She wouldn't talk to him about her brother, would she? Ever. She wouldn't name him or admit how much she thought about him. Marriage wouldn't break the isolation. She looked across at Stephen: God, she'd probably never move her lips again! And the old pain in her side, like a stitch but not a stitch, the concave bit above the waist, physical shyness and insecurity that she never felt when going anywhere, seeing anyone, at home. No time this time to forewarn Stephen; Dora got off her bike without explanation and, this time, on a track between two flat fields of those dread potatoes, she was sick.

TWO

At Carver the map of the landscape is mirrored in the set of the mouths of its people, in the sullen blankness of the eyes which inspect the stranger. Like sea anemones they pride themselves on closing up when poked or prodded. 'Repel all boarders' is engraved on the shellac of their souls. Carver Hill bears witness to their pride and their obduracy. The houses are in disrepair, the young and the talented gone. They are people on their way to self-destruct. Only the past is always with them: suicide missions, heroic defeats, half a dozen last stands . . . the grave-yard – they mow and weed it – suggests a necrophiliac adulation of the dead.

Splendid isolation keeps the memory vital, freezing weather keeps it fresh, hope – that demented, speech-less, nine-year-old Frere twin, who picks his nose until it bleeds and wears his cap backwards, might, in time, make a new leader? – lies thin on the ground.

In a terrace of cottages cut into the hillside, a terrace in which only the central three remain standing and even these are shored up from the outside with heavy wooden props, Nat Lydney, Carver to the very bone, admires his reflection in the glass. He is wearing one of Stephen's jackets, it fits him rather well.

'You look better in it than he does,' the cigarette voice of Pam Jukes whom he can see in the mirror behind him, propped up in bed, the double bed filling the room, the heater on full blast.

'He won't miss it,' she adds.

He liked the first comment but the second irritated him, no one likes to be reminded of being second place. He kicked the clothes he had taken off her, where they had fallen to the ground the night before.

'Why don't you get this place cleared?' disentangling his toe from the shoulder strap of her slip. He would have laughed at that one time; he might have picked the slip up, held it in his arms and smelt it. Now he just folded the jacket – he was horribly neat – folded it, put it over the back of a chair, sat down on the sagging double bed to put his boots on.

'Nat,' she cooed, leaning forward, her breasts hanging white above the covers, but he got up and out of range to get the second boot on.

'I've got to go.'

'Kiss me,' she called, hopping up and leaning over the wooden banisters of the narrow stairs. He kissed her, not a brilliant kiss. She could still get him, but only just. She gauged it on her own scale, knowing more than most of the waxing and the waning of these things.

Nat Lydney doesn't live with Pam, he just visits her when he wants her and he wants her less and less. He lives, sparely, compactly, in the other terrace down by The Bottoms, though he has his eye on Stephen's house. His eye a bird's eye, his head a bird's head, his step a bird's step on the ground. Only Morality, Pam's daughter, dares to mock him. Sitting in the dark corner where he wouldn't notice her, her voice, 'Fits nice, does it?' comes out of nowhere as he goes downstairs, startling him.

Nat will wear the jacket to the wedding, the wedding which has put Morality in a mood. She crashes about downstairs after he leaves, making coffee for her mother. Water boils, steaming up the grubby little window panes; Morality goes through her mother's handbag for the cigarettes.

'Morality,' her mother calls.

'Coming!'

Probably too much to hope that Dora would be old and ugly, fat?

'Effin wedding,' Morality intones.

'You promised to do Mrs Pierce's hair this morning.' Her mother again.

'All right!'

Still she slouches about downstairs, putting on her make-up at the kitchen table, it's the only place that's warm. Stubbing her cigarette out in the empty packet of ten, there'll be ructions over that. She has shaved her eyebrows – she shaves everything – and painted in their place an expression that makes her look permanently surprised.

'I started shaving my arms too,' she told her friend Maggie, the Frere twins' elder sister. Shaving was a reaction to her mother who, though still a young woman, had for some time been peculiarly attached to her dressing gown, its lapels with cigarette holes, grease marks, and other marks and stains particularly around the back.

The dressing gown appeared now, gave her an affectionate shake, made two cups of coffee.

'Don't forget Mrs Pierce now.'

'I won't.'

Morality has everything set, mended, ironed for what she is going to wear for tomorrow's wedding, but doubts her mother has done the same. She has to be on to her mother all the time in case she let her down. After Mrs Pierce's she will come back and go through her mother's stuff and make a few suggestions. She paved the way to mention this.

'Morality!'

'I'm going now.'

No one cared about Morality's schooling. It went right past Pam, who'd been tied up in a series of affairs. Morality is fifteen, her only job thus far has been to look after Alice, Stephen's mother, at the big house. With Alice dead, life is pretty boring; Maggie Frere, the only other girl around her age, is working down at the general store, The Rinkha, at Midway. Morality has time to spare, but no one to share it with. She shaves a lot, she kicks around with the twins. Regardless of the weather, her approach is heralded by a peculiar, tap, slide, tap – high heels of Alice's, far too big.

Morality's got a lot of Alice's things, by fair means and foul. She'd lived up at the big house to look after Alice, slept in the adjoining bedroom so she was ready to leap up at any time through the night. Alice drinking gin in that cold bedroom. Morality wouldn't touch a drop but she got rid of the evidence, they were friends. A proper friendship, a two-way friendship, not like the bossing she got from Maggie, not like playing with the twins. Alice gave her things, the best was a hardback book with colour illustrations, *In Search of Charm*, but it wasn't what Alice gave her or what Morality had taken, it was talking with Alice that was the best bit, talking with Alice like a proper friend. Sorting out stuff with Alice, being all domestic, poking about in her cupboards and that in the happy hour when Alice was not too sober, not too drunk. It was Alice who'd planted the idea of how Morality might make money.

'Women will always want to be made more beautiful, Morality. You can't go wrong with that.'

Touching all Alice's stuff, talking like an adult. Alice suggested the card, Alice made Stephen write it, Maggie – reluctantly, for she was always jealous – placed the card in the window at The Rinkha:

'Morality Jukes of Carver Hill. Beautician, hairdresser, manicurist.'

There wasn't much left of Mrs Pierce's hair. One didn't so much do it as arrange it around the head and all the time she worked on it, Morality kept one eye open for Dora. The road was dressed, black cattle munched on hay thrown in on top of a frozen field, the hooter that blasted out the shifts of the cement factory in Midway sounded, smoke rose in the cold air from the cottage chimneys. The sky turned yellow, livid, and in the fading light faces kept watch at their windows to see Stephen and his future wife arrive.

'Medium height,' said Mrs Pierce, 'long nose.'

'Red nose,' Morality corrected her, and, god not another one, 'thin hair.'

They came in through what Dora supposed to be the back. Stephen took her upstairs, showed her their rooms, adjoining, and suggested she might like to change and, somewhat doubtfully, that there should be hot water. Change, he would change as well he said. Oh! thought Dora, this was it then. Let's both change was a euphemism, obviously. He'd mentioned tea but that would be afterwards, after he had come through to her bedroom . . .

Time was of the essence. Dora rocked with nerves. She washed her hands in the little cracked basin tucked into a corner of the room; she brushed her teeth vigorously to get rid of the smell and taste of sick. Hurrying, hurrying, lest he might come in. Her hands shook as she splashed some scent on, the top of the bottle rolled off beneath the bed. The carpet – it had been his mother's room – smelt of recent death. There was a single electric light of very dubious wattage. She combed her hair in front of a pretty feminine mirror, a crumbling gilt frame ornamented by a single cherub who had lost his foot. Combed her hair then messed it up again as combing had made it go haywire. No middle way with Dora's hair, wetting the edge of a towel and damping it down – oh this was awful – just made it look flat. It was freezing in the bedroom. Her heart beat wildly: change, that's what he'd said. She stood about in her underclothes in the freezing room and waited, expectantly, for that noise from romantic novels, the thoroughly male sound of his approaching boots. She struck several poses in front of the mirror, breasts out, bottom tucked in; sat, a bit uncertainly, on the slippy bedspread looking at herself in the cloudy glass.

No approaching boots, no purposeful, very male, eagerly approaching boots despite the fact that even in the weak light – perhaps because of it – she felt she looked, apart from her hair, as good as it was possible for her to look. No sound, no sound except the slithery noise she made as she got on and off the bed. The water trickling down old pipes when she pulled the brass plug of the little basin, death and deathly quiet.

How long was it before everything just sagged? At what point did she begin to notice how her head ached from the cold and being sick? Rigid with cold now, so much time passing that perhaps it would be better to stay here, too embarrassing to go and find him; which was worse? Dora's teeth were chattering and she felt she'd failed. She dressed herself and found her way to where he was sitting, waiting for her, cup in hand and rather puzzled by the long delay.

Everything pointed to past glories, even in her state she saw that. The mirror's broken frame, the wide bare boards of the corridors and the landing. The Childes who'd built this settlement two hundred years ago, who'd established Midway and New Mills, must have been something; Stephen, the last of them, supping tea from a cracked cup.

They sat in two heavy chairs upholstered with tapestry. The backs were carved with representations of the four seasons, autumn's sweet chestnuts particularly uncomfortable on the back. A word or two about milk and sugar, no sex.

He was looking fixedly out of the long windows; she felt she had lost all touch of who he was. There were opened letters on the tray; why he should want to read anything now, how could he see to read in such an awful light? Mortally embarrassed by the mistake of waiting for him, the mistake seemed to sound loud – anything would sound loud – in this silent house. So Dora yawned extravagantly, rubbed her eyes, but very carefully, she wouldn't smudge her make-up, and began to tell a tale about how she'd had a little nap on the bed, so comfortable, how really tired she was.

'I can sleep anywhere,' she lied.

Who was this man and what was the matter with him? Didn't he have any idea? Whatever his thoughts were it seemed impossible to break into them, to move with him from one layer to another. He showed her the ceiling of painted angels; she looked up at it for a long time. He might notice, find irresistible, the whiteness of her neck?

They talked about the ceiling – he said this was his favourite room. How it was this room he had longed for when he had been away, how he liked to sit here like this and watch the twilight, he called it 'the shut of the day', only she'd missed the twilight, more embarrassment, the yellow sky had long gone, it was now completely dark. And she had planned to be a waterfall that evening, well so much for that. She was the trickle of water gravity pulled down the old lead pipes, she was a tiny tinkling sound in the silence, the music of the brook in the background, the tea pouring into the cup.

THREE

At first light on his wedding day Stephen clambered up a short-cut track to the church, dipping his head beneath the wet holly branches on the overgrown path. Up, up into the hummocky sea of the graveyard and the road dressed beyond it, the dark green of fir and yew against the frosted ground. Mist still topped the hill where the sheep were grazing, and beyond the churchyard wall, broken and bowed where chaotic trees had slung their branches, the blurred shapes of a herd of tough black cattle. An iron cross marked his mother's grave and then all around him the sea of the graveyard, up and down, and he alone in it, relishing the combined smells of cattle, hay, yew and fir, wet and dripping wood.

He came up here by instinct rather than design. The importance of the death–blood, of the graveyard, had been well and truly drilled into him as a little child. Carver people would consider such communing – the groom on his wedding day – quite appropriate. Dedication of his unborn children to the cause? Thank God they weren't mind readers, for this wasn't what he thought at all.

He came up here by instinct rather than design but his instinct was to ignore the dead, to confer with other gods. The way his mind ran these days surprised him, for here, in this cold somewhat forbidding setting, he found himself, almost despite himself, negotiating for a second chance.

At sixteen he'd been part of the group that set fire to Angelo's Bar Café. It burnt out, on that occasion, and three top men were caught in the inferno. In those days their intelligence was scrappy, they'd planned a warning and had scored a coup. What happened at Angelo's was something of a sensation, one of many watersheds, turning points, long overtaken by subsequent events. And after Angelo's, Stephen had to keep his head down to survive. He left Carver but Carver continued to look after him; the money wasn't regular but he could survive on it. What began as a new life that he could make nothing of because of homesickness, became with time something he could accommodate, something he might even enjoy.

Letters from home delivered in the morning, letters he didn't bother to open until the evening, letters to which replies were ever shorter, letters to which he no longer bothered to reply at all. The local paper which his mother forwarded, folded in on itself, left unopened; a sense that Carver Hill could no longer really reach him, a growing frustration with the whole damn thing.

The freedom of the loose end in another place with new preoccupations suited him well in his twenties, but as his third decade approached his fate began to seem rather a raw deal. The antics of those around him seemed stale now and increasingly soulless and the sense of loss he'd felt at the beginning returned with double strength. The doctor who'd pronounced him A1 fit talked of troubles of the heart perhaps? Troubles of the heart, yes, and troubles of the soul. Craving, always craving; relationships with women that hit the buffers when it came to children, for the children of his imagination . . .

The children of his imagination were the children other cultures catch in flickering cine film. Children pottering with a watering can in a garden full of flowers, children with a glass of milk beside a guarded fire. His children, whooping as they ran along the angel gallery, born in the bedroom with the cherub mirror, baptised in the church where he now stood.

His mother had died in November, November filled the tanks with rain. Wet and dank November, water overflowing from blocked gutterings, water coursing down the unmade road from Carver Hill. Morality, who made him smile with her shenanigans, Maggie Frere who offered something else. Alone in the empty house, just the sound of his footsteps, the slowness of the life here, the unhurried possibility of going back to childhood things. Maggie came to see him on those misty, darkening, late autumn afternoons. Stood with her back to him at the long windows in the room with the ceiling of the painted angels. Looking out across the garden walls towards The Sevens. Maggie's twin brothers playing in the dusk where the big barn doors divided up the terrace of cottages. Watching as they set a pile of the stones that old Amy Lind had placed with pride around her garden. Amy Lind a figure from his childhood, long dead, her white stones used for children's play. They said those stones had come from the very edge of the sea, they

27

were all rounded, not a rough surface on them, not like the flint of the upland stones. Round white stones, darkened by the rain, embedded in the mud. Open the casement just a fraction and the sounds and smells came into the long room; the smell of smoke and cooking, the sound of the factory hooter from Midway, the caw of rooks in the Scotch pines he had longed for. Sounds and smells that Maggie and Stephen had grown up with.

Now the twins were up on one of the hinges of the great barn doors, taking turns, clinging to the latch and standing on the iron for a ride. Stephen drinking his tea and the squeak of the barn door and the cup going down on to the saucer. How he came and stood behind Maggie, putting his cold hand up the back of her clothing, round to the front where he cupped her breast and felt the nipple and felt the nipple till it stuck out and she leant back against him and he thought as he did this of what a farmhand might do to a chicken; of playing with the Pierce boys in the barn. The Pierce boys with catapults and penknives, of that part of childhood and this time of dusk. Of how they taught him to pick a chicken up, put its head beneath its wing, then turn it slowly round and round and round and round until it became disorientated. Then, to put it gently down on to the earth, see, how it will stand there more than bewildered, hypnotised. And Maggie Frere limp against him, limp beneath the blue ceiling with its angels, as he stood now stroking, now tweaking her nipple, the squeaking of the barn door, the children playing on at the shut of a winter's day.

Coming home, the best autumn in the west that

anyone could remember. His mother seeing none of it, hysteria with a bottle in her hand. Holding on to the furniture, pulling herself around the upstairs of the house, cursing everyone in shouting distance, particularly Maggie's mother, Netty Frere. Pulling herself around the upstairs of the house, then crawling – only a son who's witnessed this knows how terrible it is – then calling him when she heard his tread on the stairs.

She put lipstick on and the lipstick missed her mouth.

'They'll come and kill us in our beds!' A shifting They that she had long lost touch with.

'That's not why I came back.'

'You don't know the half of it.'

And she was right in a way, for a new They soon came creeping. Nat Lydney was the one. Explaining to Stephen as if he could have forgotten how society worked down in the west. He asked for a backhander, on a regular basis, payable at the beginning of each month.

'You don't know the half of it.' It didn't take him long to get the gist. Nat was running a protection racket.

'I assure you Stephen that it's nothing else.'

A protection racket that kept the right people in the right houses, which gave them the right jobs. Everyone was into something, it was self-defence. It was the price you had to pay down here, it sorted things out and kept them sorted, that was all it was.

'This payment means we're right behind you Stephen, makes you one of us. You won't have to lift a finger.'

Only sign a cheque.

Holding the hand that couldn't put the lipstick on, talking nonsense about the future.

'Is it your birthday?'

Should he say no or yes? Listening to her breathing, 'Children Stephen, that nice girl you used to lodge with, Dora Parks?'

Stephen lingered in the graveyard sniffing up the wet smell of the frozen wood. The air so cold like a black dog on your back, Carver in the morning. Bright December, wide, high sky for this his wedding day. No one was going to kill anyone in their beds, that side of things was over. Just a little down payment, easy terms, 'For your children and your children's children. See it as an insurance, Steve.'

A deal between old mates.

The hummocky land of the graveyard, the field barn high on the horizon, the bleached hills and frozen earth. He loved it with the passion of someone who had almost lost it, he hated it with the passion of someone who had been made to pay. The up and down sea in which the dead lay buried, where natural causes were tantamount to sacrificing yourself to the right side. Carver dead, implacable, the glorious who had fallen and the man who stood among them on that winter morning; the man whose children ran along the angel gallery, played in peace around the monkey puzzle tree, the man who would roll the sea back, move the mountain, make the river run uphill.

Morality woke to the sound of Nat and her mother at it in the next door bedroom.

'Effin B!' she grabbed the clothes laid out for the wedding and went to dress down with Mrs Pierce.

'What's cookin?' asked Albie, the talker of the twins who picked up every new expression.

'Effin rabbit Albie, effin bloody B!'

In Search of Charm lacked a section on the revitalising of old peasants, so it was touch and go. Morality made little rushes at Mrs Pierce's face with a great powder puff. Though only just into her seventies, her client looked raddled. Walt, husband of blessed memory, had been killed 'cut in two, that's what I heard' in an accident at the cement works when her children were still young. Signs of the work she'd done to keep them, and keep them still, unmarried and middle aged now, ran as deep in her face as the rivulets down Carver Hill.

Pasting powder on her cheeks only made the lines seem deeper, 'gently does it then', she tickled the hairy nostrils with her puff. Morality banned eye-shadow, 'too crepey'; Mrs Pierce studied her face in the mirror; 'all natural talent', Morality said delving deep into what she called her overnight. This travelling case had been given her by Alice, all the rest was nicked. Tweezers, pincers, lash curlers, tubes without tops on, bottles without lids; a cherished, tiny, round, blue, cardboard box of Bourjois rouge. She smoothed a tiny bit of this on Mrs Pierce's leather cheeks. Potions gone hard, scent gone putrid, cuticle remover, nail scissors, nail hardeners. The tortoise-shell brush and comb set with its initials A.O.C. were the most valuable theft and were kept hidden in a soft, pale blue leather pouch which read 'Pyjamas' also appropriated, stuffed into a recess of the wall of the barn between The Sevens.

Mrs Pierce soaked her hands in warm lemon water. This was a token gesture – the hands were wire wool out of floor cloth; she had been given a blunt knife and an undersized potato to practise on in her pram. Morality paused for another cigarette. Netty Frere looked in to see how Mrs P was going on.

Carver had plenty to say already about Dora: Morality got the gossip fresh. Thin hair and a figure that was only average, Dora spoke stuck up; her eyes were nice but her face was pointy, her nose was rather long. She had quite looked through Netty's Maggie. Almost everyone did this but that was not the point. It was easy to establish the point: Dora came from town. She was from somewhere else, people who came from somewhere else . . . Morality drifted into coma as the two older women yacked on and on.

People who came from somewhere else were barbarians. To know how people ought to be one had to look no further than Mrs Pierce's sons, to look at Ralph and Frankie who had never been further than Midway. Away changed and altered things that mattered, it made people discontented, it diluted home. Mrs Pierce remembered, or thought she did, a time, long gone, when youngsters were quite happy to stay put.

'Not that there wasn't always the odd one . . .'

'Himself,' said Mrs Pierce referring to Stephen.

'Ah, but that was different altogether,' Netty reminded her, but Mrs P was on her hobbyhorse and wouldn't be bucked off by exceptions.

'Going off and coming to no good.'

Morality did Netty's nails next, capable, mole hands. Netty was a tireless cook and gossip: give Netty a morsel of food or information and she could turn it into something else. Carver through and through and proud of it, Netty came from a long line of superstitious dabblers and fancied her chances as soothsayer of the west. Netty saw things, put two and two together, frog and bat. A peculiar cloud formation, the cry of an owl, the consistency of an afterbirth were meat and drink to Netty Frere. And, on this point, Netty wasn't happy with the feel of this forthcoming wedding, she wasn't happy . . .

Doing well somewhere else amounted to coming to no good, and listening to the two of them hard at it you could believe that no one else was any good. The world, small enough as it was, dwindled to the people in that kitchen. Ralph and Frankie presented themselves to their mother in shiny suits, necks begging freedom from celluloid collars; their red working hands could have done with a powder too. Talk, talk . . .

Talk, talk . . . the same ones who had been at Alice's funeral now turned out to see Stephen wed. Talk, talk, conversations continued unabated in the church and Dora heard them in the background, a hum like bees in a roof, waves on shingle. This was it and it felt like play-acting, nothing to confess. A grisly little priest shuffled up to the altar, she felt the press of congregated Carver at her back. Congregated Carver, a set of teeth welded together, she felt them like a single block. In the colourlessness of the day they were parchment coloured, wax and smells of rosemary and bay, the cream of the stone, candles and cold daylight.

The priest mumbled hopelessly, everything about him suggesting that though he stood before them he had no wish to attract their attention; speed mumbling, for someone might break the church door down at any minute, his shoulders hunched against the blow he imagined from the back. Carver chatted on regardless as the host was raised above them, they had no fear of God. A miserable performance from the priest, few ups and downs or intonations, ritual gestures done very quickly, palms face outwards, face the congregation, turn away from it, frayed vestments, ingrained cuffs.

'May God join you in one.'

'Cut in two, that's what I heard.' Mrs Pierce flanked by her two unmarried sons. To her, the priest's voice was like a cart rumbling past as carts did in her childhood, and the bells of the mass were the latten bells one cart rings as warning to another on a narrow lane. Secular bells ringing in her head and her failing eyes drawn to the fusty maiden's garlands, the paper dusty and cobwebbed and as colourless as the day. The colour of the year, green and grey, the rosemary and the bay in the architraves, the colourlessness of the garlands, a tune coming into her head that Walt had sung to each boy in his turn in the cradle, *da da da dum dum da da da dum dum da da da*.

The shaking hand that raised the chalice spilt the blood. There were signs that Nat Lydney had put the frighteners on the priest; a few words it would be, their terms, and a clinching awful smile.

'Such is the blessing that awaits every man,' Netty

intuited a messy end to this beginning, a comforting sensation that made her feel all warm. Her husband Enda broke into her thoughts as husbands will; did she remember the wedding at Midway, two old boys from Gobbins imprisoned for a month for bringing a dog in underneath their coats? The twins laid out the contents of their pockets on the wooden lip of the pew in front, began to kick each other, scuffle over a boiled sweet. Dogs were par for the course these days, kneeling and standing were perfunctory; one of the twins was on the floor, a cold light through clear windows, winter morning, singing really very thin.

Dora in her dress from Bests department store: 'If your clothes aren't becoming to you, you should be coming to us.' Bloody freezing in the church, but a bride can't wear a vest.

'May the Lord who dwells in Sion bless thee: mayest thou see Jerusalem in prosperity all thy life long. Mayest thou live to see thy children's children, and peace resting upon Israel.'

She couldn't believe it, she felt a burst of happiness.

'Father Cuffe.'

'How do you do?'

The priest's hands were sweaty, Stephen's hands were cool and firm. The priest beamed with nervous relief as man and wife made small talk, waited in the porch for the congregation to line the two hundred yards of green path.

'Kinder if it would snow.'

'Too cold to snow.'

There they stood the people of Carver, coats wrapped around them, collars up, the women seeing one thing and the men another, all men seeing what Stephen saw and had decided, legally, to take. The tune from the organ playing another, round, round, round, round. Stephen's family name, Childe, all over the church – endowed by Childe, restored by Childe, sustained by Childe. Childe, the Childe insignia in the stone hands clasping one another, Stephen holding her hand in the church where his family name appeared more than the name of God of Sion, of Jerusalem.

'Get his bride back into the warm.'

Talk, talk. Some blank faced, some plain curious. Morality, on tip-toe, staring rudely; smiles these days cost more than Lydney paid for. Against Dora on principle and yet, and yet, as she walked out towards them,

'Very young.'

'Lost her brother.'

'Won't be easy.'

'Think of Alice.'

'In that barn of a place.'

Even the diehards softened as she came towards and passed them walking on the carpet of the trees, not so you'd notice mind, simply for a fraction of a second, a wedding was a wedding when all's said.

Morality with her mother, Ralph and Frankie, the scrummage for the bay bouquet which Maggie won.

Back to meet a list of names and first impressions never to be found again. They went through rooms she remembered later by their smells – straw, sacks, artichokes and apples – her feet in the little leather-soled shoes felt the cold of the brick floors. Under-used or unused sculleries, hooks in ceilings strung with cobwebs, mole traps, axes, dusty windows, baling twine and tyre chains, meal bins and potato sacks, a stone sink with a dented saucepan crusted with hen food. Stephen left her for a moment, he'd forgotten something, the smell of apples in the gloom, 'A word in your ear.'

A balding man called Tom Allen swept the cobbles with a broom. Dora pretended fascination with the line of white zinc jugs of water set on the uneven floor around the well's electric pump. Old wellingtons, overalls, boots and hats, scarves, coats, the wind through the open door.

'Would it snow?'

'Too cold for snow.'

Dora in her wedding dress. Stephen coming back, putting his hand beneath her elbow, steering her through latched doors which he nudged open, tossing his greatcoat across a wedge of old newspapers. Kindling and coal scuttles, mantelpiece above the stove, animal syringes, instructions for dosing, single rubber gloves, a rose for a watering can, indigestion powder, framed photographs all partly obscured, obfuscated, by layers of sticky dust. And then, glory alleluia! and quite unexpectedly after all this boring meeting and shaking hands and politeness and mix of smells, he led her upstairs once again through her room into his room which held a huge chair like the ones on the gallery but leather covered; his room where a fire had been laid but had not taken too well. She couldn't have a fire, he explained, something to do with the chimney smoking but she was to enjoy this fire and

37

could have it in as long as she wanted, 'A small room like this heats up very quickly.'

And she knew what was coming as he hovered over the poker, went to the window and then back again and his voice saying this and that, repeating himself, warming his hands by the fire like a doctor and her toes quite numb and flat-feeling in her leather slippers. He put his hands around her waist. Should she say it now, 'I love you'? Sat her on the chair and looked at her. He undid his own clothes and lifted up her wedding dress, the hands she'd wanted for so long, soft on the bones of her hips and an armful of petticoat, his face in her neck, his hands smoothing the bodice of her dress.

'Undo yourself, undo yourself.'

Mumbling into her ear and squashing her against the back of the chair, where she sprawled like a doll that can't sit up, like a doll – is this meant to be enjoyable? – that had an arm now stuck between its legs. And then. Again. More gently. On top of the bed where lay his discarded clothes, on the top of his jacket that smelt like the downstairs rooms – of straw and sacks and artichokes and apples – and the smell of the bedroom, lavender and mothballs from the cupboards, gin? The call of a cockerel, the bark of a dog, and Tom Allen's voice outside and slow feelings inside of something wonderful, the bud of love now that they were married.

Nothing was fair. Morality played on the barn door stoop with the twins.

'Pass us your donkey with the dent in it. Give us that lady with the rolled up sleeve.'

She let them have a go with her things, play havoc with the contents of her overnight. Allowed them to line up her nail polishes, to rank them like soldiers, to put them to bed in old cigarette packets lined with cotton wool.

'Careful mind!'

Boys annoyed her. Morality kept up a monologue as she played with them, 'Bloody, bloody, effin B!' the words her mother said.

As soon as she showed an interest in their things, an interest – by that she meant a better way to play the game – the three-legged dairy cow, 'Lean her up against something why don't you?' they'd go right off the boil, start to muck about. Playing fivesies with the stooks of corn, the little lead hens, the tiny pig troughs, throwing pebbles at her varnishes.

'Do that and I stop playing.'

'We're not playing anyway!'

Off they went to go climbing trees up at the churchyard. Morality didn't want to dirty her good clothes and she didn't want to go all over just this minute, Dora might come out of the house.

'Dora! Dora!' they taunted her.

She hung on for another sight of Dora but Dora didn't come. Maggie had caught the bay bouquet, life was so unfair. Morality went to bed that night in cotton gloves soaked in hand cream, protection for hands itching for some satisfaction. Hands eager to get back at anyone, preferably the twins, hands prepared to do a lot of hitting, slapping, scratching, pinching, Chinese burning . . .

Night, and Father Cuffe returned to civilisation on

his Lambretta, his trust in God bolstered by the protection granted him on this dreaded visit so far off the beaten track. Lydney cannot stomach Pam tonight, Pam sleeps on her own, but the curtains are drawn at Stephen's place, keeping the heat in the room; the wedding dress and the petticoat on the floor of the bedroom where Dora and her lover lie beneath the slippery bedspread softly and peacefully asleep.

FOUR

Newspapers thrown from the bus that brings cement workers in from New Mills are lugged across to the Midway shop, The Rinkha, by a boy employed by its proprietor, Big Don. The boy is far too small for the load. He drags the papers along the puddled ground; Big Don shouts from his place on the high stool by the counter but he doesn't move. Later he slips a knife under the twine and frees the bundle: headlines speak of peace to come. Big Don stacks the copies on the counter, taking the dirty wet one for himself, turns the limp and filthy pages until he gets to what he's interested in, boxing news.

Peace is billed as the answer to everything. Pam Jukes is not so sure. Nat's as picky with her over Christmas and the New Year as he was in those first bad weeks of autumn when Stephen Childe came back. Pam does everything Nat asks of her but nothing's going right.

'He'll come round,' says Maggie Frere, but Pam knows different, doesn't think he will. He comes and goes these days, he won't make arrangements: 'Expect me when you see me.' Pam can count on one hand the number of times since Stephen's wedding that Nat has stayed the night.

'Everyone's on edge just now. You know they are.'

Maggie again, all peace talk, but what difference will peace make to the likes of Pam? Maggie is full of rumours from Midway, she takes after her mum. Peace-keeping forces moving westwards at a lick, 'Fresh faces,' she tells Pam encouragingly.

'Where there's life there's hope.'

Dora has none of Pam Jukes's problems. She is absolutely in love with her new husband, she trails him round the house. She brings him coffee and finds his cigarettes for him; when he goes out she asks at what time he might like some tea. Her thoughts are full of him. She feels she has some power over him, feels that when he is preoccupied, worried by the news or the weather or whatever he worries over, that she can tease him out of it, just by touching him, on the arm, along the back. She can make her eyes appeal to him, she can be persuasive; she blows kisses at him through the windows, tries to make him blush. 'I want you to feel absolutely free Dora.' She would make him feel that he was absolutely caught.

Her thoughts were full of him, she adored more than his back. She wanted to sit on his knee, live in his pocket, lie in his arms along a sofa. She wanted to be with him, to sit by him, to talk to him, she wanted the day to be just like the night. Let day be night for the day was difficult for Dora, the silence of the place he'd brought her to was truly awful, you could hear the grasses grow.

Carver, what a dump he's brought her to. Gazing out of the window she is less than gripped. The sagging ridge-line of thatch along The Sevens, derelict cottages, abandoned pieces of machinery, broken gates, banty hens picking among the remains of a brick chimney. Sheep moving along the skyline on tracks almost perpendicular, one behind the other, single file. Sometimes Tom Allen, the day labourer, sends a dog racing after them. This is an event.

The works hooter from Midway punctuated the outside world at 8 a.m. and then again at 4 p.m. The inside world shuddered to the sound of the well's electric pump.

To entertain herself she likened what she saw to opera. The principals, all male, were to be observed, preening and striking poses, from the back windows of the house which overlooked the yard; focusing on the yard gate was recommended for a young woman not otherwise engaged. The yard gate, the spot on the stage where fatties in tights wag their beards a bit, exchange important information; a cockerel with Bumble Foot, 'Don't like the sound of that!' Nat Lydney and Tom Allen, one gesticulating, the other standing as if planted in the ground. Ralph and Frankie Pierce on their way back from the cement works, Lydney with the postman, real excitement; Lydney with Stephen, Stephen's shirt tail hanging at the back, Lydney very springy and tucked in.

Women, apparently at one with one another, jostled at the well side, giggled and made faces behind their hands. Dora recalled the infuriating tripping feet and trilling voices of the operatic chorus, gathered skirts, embroidered bodices, baskets of paper fruit and flowers, 'What will be the fate of young Julietta

43

when she discovers Giovanni in the arms of someone new?'

Plucking dummy chickens while minions added the final touches to the principals in their dressing rooms, a pretty backdrop, pretend smiles, pretend gossip, rhubarb, rhubarb, the chorus of Carver women went about their work.

Morality, often with a cigarette in her mouth, always in high heels, brought her mother's washing in, stiff with frost. Mrs Pierce threw tea leaves round her garden, 'Tra la la'; Netty swept her step with vigour; Maggie came out with something in her apron for the hens. Women cut kindling, carried logs, had a quick word across the gardens, 'Oh, I fear the outcome of this fearful day!'

A shout to a husband in a far-off field, 'Luciano, hail!'

Crying children, a dash for the Germolene, 'Come hither and nestle in the folds of my dirndl skirt.'

Barking dogs, cackling hens, monstrous cockerels, rooks bounce landing underneath the plum trees. Day so difficult for Dora, stuck-up voice, stuck up in the dress circle, she didn't have a part. An animal grazed, a banty pecked, a man put his lips around a spark plug; she needed an excuse to walk about. Stick, bucket, broom or basket, jump leads, hay bale, fodder – Dora couldn't go outside, she didn't have a prop. She needed a hen to chase or a bucket to carry, or something to shout into the raw, cold air.

Help?

Two fairly awful things struck Dora in the first weeks of her marriage; Stephen did not think that life at

Carver was at all peculiar – this was number one. The second was that she had moved, unwittingly, into the world of lavender bags and jam.

Dora addressed an envelope to her father in the hope of slipping something suitably incriminating into it at a later date: a photograph of her yoked up with an ox? Carrying a loaded firearm? Downing a glass of spirits with a wanted man? She carried this envelope with her on her first sortie; should her prop-less movements be questioned, she could confound the chorus by saying she was going to the post. She expected to be challenged, savages, it was well documented, having eyes in the backs of their heads. She held the letter in a glove that probably, in their eyes, looked too new; walked, she could remember how to do that, walked down to the allotments, The Bottoms, for a scout about. Nothing here but cabbages and the green tops of things she didn't recognise – parsnips, swedes? One of the twins – she realised soon enough it was the dark demented one – joined her in this progress. When she spoke to him he picked up a stone and made as if to hurl it at her.

'Watch it!' The strange sound of her own voice had much the same effect on him as a small tranquillising dart on a rhinoceros. He looked quizzically at her but he didn't leave her; he stuck by her looking threatening, kicked the stone in front of them as they walked.

'Must have seen you setting out,' Mrs Pierce, hatchet face, speckled with blackheads. 'All eyes that one.'

'Usen't to be houses left like that.' A scrawny arm pointed to the devastation. Dora's eyes fixed on the

45

woman's stick legs, on the stockings that looked as though they weren't properly held up.

'Cold even with a roof on when you haven't got the heat from them on the other side of you,' now pointing out her own place in the terrace.

Dora clutched the empty envelope. The child had picked the stone up again.

'Yes.'

Mrs P defused the situation this time, pulling the boy roughly to her side. She seemed rather taken with him, 'Don't talk, this one. He's a twin.'

'Can't he talk?' Was this a giant two-year-old or an average child of nine?

'He can talk, when he's a mind to. Can't you?' She cuffed him affectionately on the head so that his hat fell off into the road, 'He can talk. The other one does the talking see. Albie.'

'That's my house,' she said, pointing again.

Dora's mother would have been horrified, it was rude to point.

Lydney cruised past in his little caddy van, Dora rather lost the thread of the conversation.

'Very cold,' she offered as a filler.

'Too cold to snow,' the old dear said.

After four on a winter afternoon and the light already going. The twin slipped off as silently as he had joined her, all at once he wasn't there. Stables turned into garages made one side of the big yard; Tom Allen, hosing the milking parlour, almost stood to attention when she said 'Hello'. He turned off the hose, was getting ready to go.

'Are you always here this time of night?'

'Hereabouts.'

'I might see you tomorrow then?' She was getting desperate.

'You might.'

'Goodnight then.'

'Goodnight miss.'

They walked in together through the first scullery that smelt of straw and apples.

'I've got some kittens if you're interested? In this press here.' He led the way towards the cupboard, opened the door then closed it quickly at the sound of a sharp tread on the cold brick floor. Lydney was behind them.

'Get off then Tom,' said Lydney.

Tom Allen four square, Lydney lighter altogether, like a bird.

Tom came from Starveall, a house on its own tucked into the hillside, went back across there every night. Now he stooped to put on each bicycle clip, a can of milk in his bicycle basket, it all seemed to take an age.

'Goodnight Tom.'

'Goodnight.'

Lydney went to the cupboard, picked up a kitten to show her. The mother spat at him, still he picked up another and another. The kittens were still blind and mewed pathetically.

'Put them back now, please. I think we really ought to put them back.'

He took his time about it. The mother hissed and spat until her family were back again; Lydney wedged the cupboard door with a bit of blanket. Tom Allen set off on his bicycle, all his movements slow and witless, turning on the lamp. Lydney so lively by comparison, something about him made her think about her waist. He was always around the downstairs of the house. If she missed the bolt of the shutter you could bet he'd be behind her, lean over her and slide the socket right.

She followed him into the kitchen, he made himself a cup of tea. This was another thing she had to get used to, sharing her kitchen with the rest of Carver Hill. They all came in and out, sat and read the paper, had some coffee and a bit of a chat. Maggie Frere, who helped when she wasn't working at The Rinkha, let slip how easy it had been in Alice's day, just a little something liquid on a tray. Mrs Pierce, who kept her hat on in the house, tucked in close to the stove, Netty helping Maggie, standing at the sink.

Stephen didn't think that this was peculiar at all. But the worst part was how they all stopped talking each time she came in, gave her sulky looks, folded their arms more fiercely across their chests. Only Morality, whom Dora was beginning to take an interest in, offered anything approaching normal human warmth.

She didn't like these women, she didn't want them in her house. She felt the weight of them monitoring her marriage, taking it all in. Even Morality's mother, who never came into the kitchen but could be glimpsed now and then kicking the cat out, even she slipped her warning looks. The weight of them, clamming up each time she walked in. Once and only once she mentioned this to Stephen, 'They sort of won't let me in,' she told him.

Stephen, realising that Dora was a bit peculiar, 'Into what?'

Day was difficult, she held on to the night. Day and night were separate. It was the most extraordinary sensation. Often now she tried to call up in the day her feelings of the night, reliving and remembering what it felt like to be loved. Stephen looked the same but she knew he wasn't, neither of them could forget. What happened at night made them partners, tied them inextricably together. When she looked at him, or he at her – even if they didn't touch – something tautened between them.

He talked to her in bed about the world he planned, about moving the mountain and rolling back the sea. They lay on their backs and he talked to the ceiling; she knew she only had to touch him to silence him, she knew. Lying back with his hands behind his head, talking; she only had to move her foot in the bed to touch his foot. Life held no terrors when you lay like this; if only you could lie together, forever, just like this. She had only to move her leg to touch his foot, drunk with power, yet one touch and the balance shifted, for touching him touched something new inside her, the pebbles skittered, a bit of a landslip and delicious weakness as if will drained out of her, loving in its place.

Dora and Stephen: did other married couples live like this? Day so separate from night? Dora slipping down the bank into the water, pushed out across the lake, floating, no power to make her own direction, like something tiny, inconsiderable, blown by the wind on to the water, a seed falling from a bird's beak, a leaf revolving.

He talked, the little scar where he cut a tendon on his right hand, the fine black hairs on his arms. He talked, she listened, she didn't talk, the only phrase she knew by heart was that life was very short. He talked and she listened and what she didn't say began to multiply as her love for him increased.

Loving him upset her sometimes, deeply. She was careful not to mention this. She'd get out of bed instead, cover herself with a blanket, wander the rooms while he slept. Stand, rubbing the dark window with her finger, sit down in another room, wrapped up in a chair. Alabaster woman, chipped by a fall, covering up the broken bit. And he would have gone on talking unless she turned to him, well she thought perhaps he would, but being addicted she always turned no matter what. And right at the beginning, though more and more as time went on, she wanted him in the daytime too. Looking out of the window, loving him, taking out his tea. But day was day and night was night to her new husband. Some instinct told her to respect this.

It would have been safer not to love him quite so much, but who cared about being safe? Loving, this amazing wonder, quite apart from everyday life, day so separate from night. On it went, like hot day after hot day in the summer, resisting the temptation to wake him though she always wanted more. Yet still night and she wanted the next night to come, for the day that hadn't dawned to run out and into being with him in bed again, half listening to him talking, her hand brushing his thigh as if by accident, then, after the first touch, the sound of their breathing faster in the silence as she wound her legs around his legs.

Two

FIVE

On the evening of the twenty-first of March the peace-keeping forces, the khaki and blue of their uniforms like an olive grove on the move with a heavy sky behind it, passed through Midway on their way towards the town. Bonfires were lit all along the Sky Road, turves soaked in petrol – for they came in a terrific downpour – were stuck on sticks and waved at them. Teenagers beat sheets of tin, children were allowed to stay up late to see it, collars up and caps on backwards, waiting in the rain. Children hoisted up on their father's shoulders, keeping count and waving, then losing count and waving, at the long and long-awaited convoy of military trucks.

'PEACE' proclaimed the headlines, peace in big black letters, peace, peace, peace. Father Cuffe was greatly relieved: the PKF had come in time to save him from the horror of his lone foray to Carver for the Feast of the White Saint. Now he took the turn from Midway with much less apprehension, his Lambretta on the back of a small truck, two soldiers travelling with him for support.

The people gathered, as they'd always done, in Hooley's Field where the road to Carver meets the track across to Starveall. Congregating here to walk back up the hill behind the priest and the two soldiers, taking the long way around, along the path made green for Dora's wedding. The priest, so much more confident now that peace had been made official. Less craven than he had been, he remained essentially a creeping timid man. He gave Nat Lydney a wide berth that March morning, anxious about the timing of the ceremony, so sure he wouldn't get things right that he'd been through it several times with Stephen in the kitchen just in case.

The prayers had to last the walking pace, which, with a congregation mostly over sixty, meant plenty of space between the words. All the women wore blackthorn in their hair, Morality managed to make hers look a come-on. The men had bunches of the white, prickly-stemmed hedge plant in the button-holes of shiny suits. White flowers everywhere, white flowers in the graveyard, white flowers strewn around Alice's iron cross, white flowers placed on the Childe effigy in the Childe church.

The day was cold, with the weakest of blue skies; the twins had to look hard for the blossoms on the hedges that year. Albie, such a mouth on him, his brother in silent and demented mode again; Albie, one obscenity after another, kicking up a fuss. They decorated the plain, clear-windowed church with silver pussy willows and pale catkins, tiny white violets hardly visible above the rim of jars that once had held meat paste. The wind rising during the service bringing the first flakes of snow. Small dry flakes blowing in from the east and the sky still blue above them. In moments the white in the women's hair was covered with a paler white as they quickened their paces down the hill, white on the khaki tops and dark blue trousers of the soldiers, the priest trotting between, clutching his vestments to his chest.

Snow lay along the hurdles of the lambing pens, it lay on the backs of the sheep. Dusk came early as the sky became more leaden. The twins now had handfuls of it, Tom Allen brushed it in the yard, Maggie kicked it off her shoes, Netty swept it off her step. The black earth around the artichokes in the bucket by the scullery door was white when Tom Allen stooped to bring it in. White falling thickly down the cobbles, the hum of the generator, the heartbeat of the yard. Amy Lind's white stones looked dirty against it, rook steps in the graveyard were defined by it, and then softened by it, as it thickened; it lay in stripes along the pale weatherboarding of the church. Morality absolutely hated it. She dug out Alice's white fur muff with the tassels on it; 'Effin snow!' It made her hands red raw. The twins cried when they called inside, had to be called three times or more, Netty shouting, 'Tea!'

By evening it was several feet deep and the sky that night prickled with definition, each star brighter and the sound of owls, the male calling to the female, the female answering the male, and the bleating of the sheep and the call of foxes, the moon serrated. Snow piled on the window ledges and in the gutters, snow obliterating the ditches, piled up high against the hedge; snow drifting through every gate and gap.

Stephen and Dora read the paper together in bed that night, PEACE in large black letters and photographs, 'Here They Come'. Junior Hall, who'd protested loudly in his youth that he'd been born a poet, had taken over from his father as proprietor of *The Tribune*. His editorial on peace showed him in full lyric mode, 'What does peace feel like? It feels as if you have been chosen. As if your generation has been singled out to start again. As if the sun has broken through, warm on your head and your shoulders and your back, and you can take your coat off now, be certain. Peace is round . . .' Dora questioned this '. . . it bounces, you can toss it high up into the air and catch it, its felicity. The murmuring of the underground river is drowned out by jubilation. The future, hidden for so long, now unrolls before you as far as the eye can see it, a green road.'

A green road – the only bump along it a cartoon showing the western part of the country as a baby wrapped in a shawl being offered a dummy by a young soldier, above the caption, 'Peace at Last'.

Peace at last. It was four months since they'd been married. Night, and night this time extended into day. For Stephen was celebrating and his optimism knew no bounds. He turned to Dora in the morning and later, in that snow-blanketed day, bringing the wood upstairs himself to bank her morning fire, they lay in front of it together, then stood together by the window looking out at the white breast of the hillside beneath a dirty sky.

It snowed little on the second day but on the second night it came again faster and more furiously, this time with a wind behind it, scooping up the first fall, carving it into fantastic shapes. The village was cut off from Midway, Tom Allen was marooned at Star-

58

veall, the works hooter sounded the shifts but neither Ralph nor Frankie stirred.

Loving under a mound of bedclothes, Dora imagined that her calls could be heard like the owls calling to each other across the night in the special silence that snow brings to the countryside. All her senses sharpened, the love – like the opposite of a poison – flowed down her arm into the fingers of her hand. She went to bed first and when he got in beside her they turned to one another straight away and he was inside her, loving her, not this time in a soft, familiar way, but as if they were compelled and bound, as if the combination of snow and peace had taken them one stage beyond themselves, but taken them together. She lay beside him. One hand beneath the pillow, the other arm, rising and falling a little, across his chest. He had become something so needed to her, four months.

She woke, perhaps some sound awoke her, extricated herself from Stephen and the bedclothes, found a dressing gown in the darkness, stood by the side of the window looking out into moonlit white. In the silence, only his breathing, her heart raced and jumped. She was frightened. Frightened by a long path, by a narrow vee? She tried to catch the coat-tails of her dreams, something with the feel of steel, the wedge with which Netty's husband, Enda, split his logs?

'Dora,' said Stephen as she climbed in beside him, as she tugged at her share of the bedclothes. 'Dora,' before going back to sleep. She wanted to say a great many things about shapes that frightened her and yet, not telling being the nature of the married state, said simply, 'Will it snow again tomorrow, do you think?'

SIX

The peace-keeping forces come to Carver in the darkness of the morning. Their lorry clatters up the unmade road, churning old snow to slush, gears racing as if trying to wake the dead. It's a quick in-and-out job, more a political exercise than one of need; ostensibly, as an occupying force, they have come to collect their percentage of the milk.

The PKFs, who are trained and paid to fight and win, get all of a fidget when their hands are tied. A mixture of career soldiers and conscripts nearing the end of their second year of service, their progress westwards has met with little opposition; their inclination is to strut a little, to throw their weight about a bit. How bored they are, stuck in this god-forsaken western region, confined each morning and each afternoon to the function room of the hotel. Lectures, lectures: lectures for their instruction and their safety; the well-informed soldier is the one who stays alive. The myriad sensibilities, allegiances, the folk myths, the family histories of the region have been condensed for them into forty-minute chunks, which is about all that they can take. The troubled history of the western region, handed out to each of them washed, ironed, pressed, flattened, like a pile of laundry. Outside forces, strangers all, brought down here to police and stabilise, instructed to be both evident and subtle, the lectures confirm to those who listen with intelligence that they are about to get it in the neck. They are bored, impatient, irritable. The hotel has not enough bathrooms and letters home speak much of the antiquity of the plumbing and the drabness of the local girls. The function room is stuffy and hot, the lecture punctuated by the sound of fortifications going up outside.

Myriad sensibilities, allegiances, criminal records, they are eager to be up and at it, to flush the bastards out. Carver is a start in this direction, cowboy country, a bit of a nervous joke. The two who've come to collect the milk watch their backs as they do so and are watched in their turn by Tom Allen, peeping between the slatting of the great barn door with a tabby kitten in his hand. They take two creamery cans left out for them the night before from the wide stone by the dairy steps. One keeps the engine going while the other drops the tailboard, loads the cans up, clunk, clunk. The operation is over in three minutes; the trickiest bit of it is backing through the gateposts into the yard. Loaded, they drive out again and down the rutted hill. They have orders that if they get a flat they must just drive on it until they reach the comparative safety of the Midway road.

Every day now opens with the noises of their operation. The PKF have imposed their own version of the dawn. Ralph and Frankie leave soon afterwards. They hear the PKF lorry heading off. 'You could set your watch by them,' Ralph says. The Pierces walk the first mile down from Carver, stamp their boots to keep the cold out, their pieces, cheese and pickle sandwiches, in the pockets of their overcoats, stamping in the half darkness of the winter morning, waiting for their lift.

PKF, PKF a set of initials on everybody's lips, a set of new rules brought in under an Allegiance Act. Peace has brought restrictions, prohibitions, rationing of petrol and gas.

'There'll be a curfew next!'

Perhaps there will. Congregation is forbidden, meetings banned, religious services suspended. All outside buildings are to be kept locked and bolted, vagrancy will from now be treated as a capital offence. New security arrangements are displayed on posters, come as supplements in the papers that the boy at The Rinkha lugs across the concrete to Big Don. Restrictions on the movement of animals mean paper work that no one's used to; identification to be carried at all times; derelict properties to be boarded up. The link between business and security is played up again and again, restrictions in order to end commercial disruption, pettifogging rules and regulations . . .

At Carver the world has changed from white back into winter grey. The hens, which stood so dubiously at the door of the chicken houses before bouncing body deep into the snow, are now chased squawking by the dominant cockerel, who sees the others off. Hens cackling over corn thrown in among the snowdrops, snowdrops at the foot of the distorted grey wood of the plum trees, bare-branched plum trees dwarfed by the hills that rise beyond them, the lay of Carver Hill.

Stephen puts both hands out to peace as if stretching for a life line. He cuts the headline, 'PEACE', out of the paper and pins it on the black kitchen dresser, an awning for the soup plates, the edges of the paper already beginning to curl up.

'Now you can offer thanks as you wash up, Dora.'

And Dora, quite seriously, says, 'I will.'

Stephen knows exactly what he's going to do with peace and makes sure that no one is in any doubt about it. He stands for peace, for compromise, if that's what the others want to call it, an end to cavilling at least. Frustrated as the next man by the new restrictions, he will go along with Special Powers, as – he repeats it again and again to those around him – a means to an end. He's going to put the houses to rights at last in Carver; he's going to plant the orchard that his mother planned, the orchard she envisaged in the lee of the hill down at Hooley's Field.

He's going to start with The Sevens and put the place to rights. When the weather improves, he will rethatch the lot. He can hardly contain himself, can hardly dare to think of all the possibilities of peace. Children running in the angel gallery, children playing round the monkey puzzle tree. Dora will have enough children to fill the school. No one will have to go through the horror of his schooling in the town.

'What horror? It wasn't horror. You enjoyed it. Horror? You're rewriting history, Stephen.'

'Absolutely – and about bloody time.'

Tom Allen looks long and quizzically at the word above the soup plates, perhaps he finds it difficult to read.

'Peace,' says Dora helpfully.

He is not impressed. 'Wouldn't let Lydney see that.'

'Don't be ridiculous . . .' Dora starts, then Stephen puts his oar in.

'Nat will come round when he sees there's money in it.'

But this does not impress Tom either. He's gone all sulky recently, he puts his head down like a sheep hesitating at a gate.

Lydney is astonished and appalled by Steve's reaction, really quite put out. He casts about for any rumour, any article which might discredit the new force. For lack of anything else to hand, he points out to Stephen, who's already noticed, the mess their milk lorry had made of the gatepost in the yard.

'That wall will be down.' He really loves saying it: 'One more knock like that and the whole lot'll be over.'

Netty Frere is in absolute agreement. Ideally she would have liked to pump the twins with growth hormone to get them fit to fight.

'Terrible bang it was,' she says, joining them in a hideous wrap-around apron. 'Terrible,' she goes on, making a meal of it. Stephen would like to rip the apron off and wind it around her neck.

'Get Tom to slap some white paint on it,' he suggests to Nat, 'make it more visible.'

'White paint!' Can Lydney believe what he's hearing? He wouldn't stand for such deliberate and provocative destruction of property, and nor would Netty Frere.

'Crashing about in your own yard,' she says to Stephen. The last of the Childes, he ought to be ashamed. 'Terrible bang it was. "That's never the gatepost again," Enda says to me only yesterday, crashing about in your own yard.'

You can go back, thinks Stephen, but it is always smaller and meaner than you think. Was this how it always was? Was this what he had killed for? Scoring points over the minutest thing? School in town, he had to think about it, was it a horror or a relief?

'Get Tom to slap some white paint on it,' he says, and walks away.

'I give them a month,' Nat tells Netty.

'Driving in here like lunatics,' Netty says.

Stephen is increasingly distracted. Before he can move the mountain he must rearrange the dolls' house, reorganise the people on the ground. He must explain compromise to them, persuade them that this peace is the best they're going to get. He puts his arm round Mrs Pierce, he chats to Ralph and Frankie, he seeks out Enda at the saw bench, talks to him about the future of the twins. There is money in co-operation; the days of Angelo's have passed. Talking, talking as if his life depended on it, but do they listen, will they take it in?

Lydney, like Tom, has gone silent on him. They work together on the farm but after his first few outbursts Lydney now will not be drawn. Stephen tries to provoke him into argument, and is met each time by the veil he remembers from long ago, the veil that masks the face. He works with Nat as much as possible. He's known him since childhood, there must still be some mileage left in that? They've played together, worked together, killed together. He likes the man, or at least he used to; how do you say that things look different when you've lived away? How do you explain yourself without appearing patronising? How do you temper your dreams, release them in digestible particles, little bit by little bit?

'You've gone soft all of a sudden,' Lydney had said to him on seeing peace tacked on to the dresser, implied that Dora was behind it, 'Mustn't let the girls dictate.'

In bed Stephen rehearses what he'll say to Lydney, although it's hard to concentrate with what Dora is doing to his leg.

'I want to live, Lydney.' Would that sound histrionic, out in the open standing up? 'I want to stay alive. I love this place as much as you do, but we are older now and Dora's changed things, she lies beside me, stroking the fine hairs on my legs. I don't feel the same loyalty any more.'

No, he couldn't say that. Absolutely couldn't. Understate the political side: 'I doubt it will stick but let's go along with it.' Stress the positive – grants going for co-operation, new markets opening up; peace and prosperity, like a Christmas card. Stephen is distracted; he turns his back on Dora, hopes that she will settle down to sleep. 'I've done my bit and you've done yours'? The two of them who once worked well as a unit, both on the same side.

Stephen is reorganising the dolls' house, but the Carverites are hardly as compliant as those old pipe-cleaner mice. It was like a fight with Lydney, and Stephen was not for giving up. A fight over those next few weeks, a fight picked up hour by hour, day by day when they found themselves alone together, a silent fight, an arm-wrestle of thoughts between them.

Stephen and Tom have paced out a plot for the orchard where the lee of Starveall Hill offers some protection from the prevailing wind. Now Stephen is down there with Lydney, doing some fencing to keep out the sheep. They'll either have to lose a line of trees or pace the whole thing out again: no posts can be driven into this bit, they keep hitting a seam or rock beneath the ground.

'Got to know when you're beat,' says Stephen, fed up with the rain and cold, the rain that trickles from his hat brim, down his neck.

But Lydney takes his jacket off, despite the downpour, hangs the jacket on a fence post, spits into his palms, the pick-axe in his hand.

The first tangible plus of occupation is that the post is operating sensibly again, a large package has arrived for Dora at Midway.

'From your parents,' says Morality, who got wind of it from Maggie.

'An olive branch?' asks Stephen, fitting a new lace into his old boots.

'Hardly.'

'They'll be coming to stay soon. Flowers on the bedside table. Tea.'

'They won't.'

'They wouldn't get the petrol,' Morality put in practically.

'Grandchildren,' Stephen says, 'a swing from the beech tree.'

Dora pulls a face at him as he nudges the kitchen

door open, tea in one hand, plans in another. 'Give me strength!'

Dora thinks she may be pregnant, just possibly, too early yet to say. She thought, after her brother died, that she'd never have a baby but since Stephen everything has changed. She wants anything now that will multiply him, and in any way. She watches him cross the yard as she drones through the washing-up. She's tired enough to be pregnant, she feels exhausted, she creates a wobbling pile of drying-up.

Morality lounges and leans in the kitchen as only a teenager can. Takes an old hairgrip out of her pocket and runs it irritatingly along the grooves of the scrubbed table, 'What's he mean, an olive branch?'

'Nothing.'

'What do you think the package is?'

'No idea,' she says, flinging the cloth, which lands half on the taps and half on the window sill.

Morality follows her upstairs into her bedroom – tap, slide, tap.

Dora feels wrecked these mornings, she can hardly catch sight of her bed without wanting to lie on it, she may be pregnant or it may just be the effort of keeping herself warm.

'You're not going back to bed again?'

'I want to have a rest.'

You could almost see Morality thinking, hear the cogs go click, click, click.

'You don't want to change these curtains, then?'

'What?'

'I been longing to change these curtains,' says Morality surprisingly. 'I wanted to swop them round ever

69

since I was looking after Alice. I like doing things about the house.'

'Well, I don't.'

'You don't mind if I change them round then?'

Dora closes her eyes. Bliss.

There comes the sound of falling plaster, 'Effin B! The pin came out the hole.' Morality walks plaster across the bedroom carpet. 'We'll have to do it now.'

'I said not to touch it.'

'No, you didn't.' She treads plaster back into the adjoining room. 'Can't you just come and look?'

Dora groans. Like something big and heavy from the zoo, she groans. Dora's mother made her own lampshades, upholstered chairs, smocked dresses, turned collars, replaced the pockets in her husband's trousers. She cleaned ovens, descaled kettles, potted meat, preserved tomatoes, rinsed ornaments in warm soapy water. She French-seamed, oversewed and hedge-tear darned; she disinfected, scrubbed, sponged, soaked, sluiced, spicked and spanned; one of her hands was pointed like a needle, the other had become a Spontex cloth. Dora groans. Morality's bright idea for a constructive morning transports them both to the world that Dora loathed with venom, the world of dustpans and brushes and searches – so often fruitless, always desperately annoying – searches for the right size of curtain rings, for a hammer and soft wood to act as a rawlplug, for screws and nails.

'Quicker to move house,' says Dora.

'You're funny you.' says Morality, collecting fragments of old plaster in her skirt.

The search for the right size of rings led them to the unoccupied bedrooms which looked out over the

yard. Shuttered rooms, fluff and dust on the raised
nails of the bare floor boards. Her mother, coming
across a room like this one, would rejoice. Iron
bedheads, old bolsters, cupboards full of folded linen,
a mouse-trap in the corner. They had forgotten the
pole to test the ring on, well of course they had;
back, forth and back again being the very essence of
domesticity, and ever-willing Morality, tap along the
passageway, tap, slide, tap. Dora opened one of the
shutters for a bit of light. A couple of men she didn't
recognise were talking to Nat Lydney in the yard.

'Vagrancy, all outside buildings, derelict properties
to be kept locked.' Why did she think of that? She
looked at the men, she looked at Nat, she wondered.

She'd had plenty of opportunity to observe Nat in
the last few months. She was in some way attracted
by what she saw. 'A bad egg' her father would have
labelled him, which was enough for her. A bad egg,
but there was something jaunty about him. She
looked at him now in the courtyard, and she couldn't
help but smile. He tried very hard to look respectable,
but somehow it never quite came off. There was
something embarrassing about his efforts: his hair so
neat, so carefully constructed below that jaunty face.
Even his working clothes looked clean and you had
to hand it to him, he had a sort of style, he cut rather
a dash. Dora often watched him, watched him eat
and drink, he never overdid it; watched him many
times as he crossed the yard, unlocked his little office
as he was doing now, the key always in the same
pocket. He was indeed as sleek as a little bird, always
alert, never quite relaxed.

They tried the pole, collected up the rings, and when Dora looked again the men had gone.

They folded the old curtains and put them in the bottom of a tall cupboard. As they came together to fold them like a sheet, Dora got a good whiff of her own scent.

'You smell nice this morning, Morality. Come here a minute.' She grabbed at her, felt in the girl's pocket. 'It's mine, Morality. Give it back!'

'It isn't.'

'If that perfume isn't back on my dressing table . . .'

'I didn't take anything.'

'If you borrow something, Morality, put it back.' She took the bottle from her. 'Honestly.'

'He probably won't try anything with you.' This in Morality's special, cynical, grown-up voice.

'What are you talking about?'

'Lydney. When he takes you down to Midway for your box.'

'You're awful,' Dora said to her, 'really awful, Morality.'

She chased her through the upstairs of the house.

Lydney drove fast in his neat little pick-up that stank of aftershave. He was showing off. They went up instead of down, right up to the field barn on the horizon. Dora enjoyed bouncing her way up the rough track; surprisingly, it was a relief to get away.

He stopped at the field barn and was gone for some few minutes. She sat coldly in the van. It was very exposed up here, bits of snow still lingered, no trees, the grass and the weed quite white with hoar frost.

Sheep gathered around the van in the hope of being fed, she was surrounded by them, nosing up against the van. Was it possible they might overturn it? Was it possible to be buffed and buffeted to death? They parted like a dirty cream sea for Lydney, back in the van now; rather awful the way he neatly pulled at the knees of his trousers each time he sat down. Was he wearing braces, surely not? Slowly he rolled himself a cigarette, didn't seem to be in much hurry. He would smile in that suggestive way. It was embarrassing being in the van like this with him, so silent and so stationary, surrounded by a sea of sheep.

'Hadn't we better be getting on.' The schoolmarm.

'No hurry,' Lothario on board.

As if wilfully prolonging the journey, he turned the engine off once they got on to the hill, coasting down.

'It's a game with me,' he said.

Sometimes the van almost stopped. 'Come on. Sort of edge it forward,' he told her. It was hard to know if he was joking. He rocked forward in his seat, he wound the window down and waved his arm like a paddle in the air. Dora really didn't know what to think. She laughed.

'You can still have fun even when you're married you know,' he said.

'Quite.'

They passed the turn to Carver, then Gobbins and Starveall; they slid silently, almost conspiratorially, down.

A group of young soldiers stood around a half-built sandbagged post on the junction with the Midway road.

'Goodness,' said Dora.

'Digging in,' said Lydney drily.

Of course he had the papers. He passed them out the window and they were waved forward casually with a gun.

In Midway other soldiers wandered freely among the workers.

'Seems a bit of a contradiction,' Dora said as they pulled in opposite The Rinkha, the shop where Maggie worked, the shop Stephen called The Mecca of the West.

'I'll see you here, all right? That's Reenie.' He pointed out a woman in a headscarf who was filling cans with paraffin. 'She'll tell you where to go.'

Midway was part of her parents' nightmare, That Dreadful Place; Dora warmed to it at once. Plumes of smoke from the cement works, a stream of stone lorries, the white of stone and the dark green of forestry plantations, terraced houses. Here too, the Childe insignia, clasped hands across the door lintels like those across the cottages and the church at Carver Hill, and the old slogan written on the road: Two for One. Here the gable ends were used for posters advertising boxing matches, clay pigeon shoots and all of it overlaid with smells of factory waste and frying coming from The Rinkha. She'd been suffering withdrawal symptoms – this was what she had been missing, a shop.

The Rinkha was more of a warehouse than a shop. Dora went towards it like a moth, the lethargy she felt at Carver sloughed right off her. Shopping! The place consisted of an enormous room that had once been a roller-skating rink for the factory hands; boxing matches still took place here periodically, but for the most part it worked as a general store, goods laid out on trestle tables around the walls. Big Don, enormous in dungarees, slumped over a counter near the entrance with the ubiquitous boxing magazine.

Dust from the works spread everywhere. It lay on the Gaiety tea-sets, the boxes of crackers, the packs of Beetle Drive, on the lavatory brushes and the gas cylinders, on the bales of material, the Sunday shoes with their laces tied together, the writing paper, the boxes of biscuits and tea. Much of what she saw was salvage stock: there would be a flaw in the material, a dent in the tin, a smudged line of print in the wallpaper; washing-up cloths hemmed only at one end, last year's colours, ends of line at the end of the line – Midway. Stock at The Rinkha didn't move, there was no time or motion, it hung around, got gradually buried as other goods were stacked on top of it by one of Don's underpaid and scrawny lads. Dust gathered along the sides of the Sellotape that crossed the bent Cellophane gift sets of hankies, each with its little ribbon bow; light faded the topmost bales of material, pins rusted in the folds of work-shirts and overalls. The stock was a balancing act of bicycle repair kits, tin mugs and plates, piece boxes, coffee pots, colanders, a jumble of unravelling face flannels and sheep-shears. Make-up and toothpaste of unknown provenance, drums of weed killer, cotton and thread, liquorice and tobacco. She recognised the notebooks Stephen had brought to school.

A corner near the road side was set out with half a dozen tables and uncomfortable settle seats built into the wall. Here Maggie Frere, behind a rough counter with cloches for currant cakes and bread and butter, fried chips and eggs and beans, made tea and sandwiches. Last year's flypaper hung from the high ceiling, the gas fridge buzzed, plastic seagull curtains half-drawn across the dusty steamed-up windows. There wasn't a breath of fresh air; it smelt of the works and it smelt of frying, of paraffin and petrol, papers and bottled gas. Dora filled her lungs with it – it smelt of life.

The package was a sewing machine. Dora might have guessed.

'Oh my God,' she recognised its shape beneath the paper. 'Christ!' Her mother never gave up, did she? What was Dora supposed to do with it? Run up a natty pair of oven gloves for the kitchen? Something stylish in sacking for herself?

Dora drank her coffee, the sewing machine beside her, in a place where her mother would never be seen dead. Beyond the window she could see the paint on the infamous gable wall – a version of Our Glorious Dead, known throughout the west as Tally Corner. It hadn't weathered well. If her brother's name was on it, she couldn't pick it out. As she watched from the café, children on their way home from school hung around it for a while, kicked footballs against it. Her brother would never stoop to hold the hand of a little child. Dora put a hand where she thought her womb was. What would her brother think of the compromise the western region had got stuck with? How would he have reacted to Stephen's about turn, to peace?

The hooter she heard at Carver blasted out now,

shift workers mixed freely and easily with the soldiers. Men white with dust were coming in for a paper, the café was beginning to fill up. Dora eased herself off the settle bench with some regret, said goodbye to Maggie. The pick-up was in the forecourt; Big Don watched her from behind the counter as she hulked the sewing machine out through the swing doors.

Morality came running out to meet them as they turned into the yard. Running out, jumping at the van like a dog, spilling over the sides of her slippers with the news. Jumping up and down beside Dora as Lydney hauled the machine out of the back.

'Dora, did you hear in Midway? Have you heard it? They found a woman hacked!'

'Who?'

Morality didn't know the name, the name was not the point. In the kitchen they put the story together as Dora, who hadn't even got her coat off yet, cleared the decks to make a cup of tea.

'Who was it?' Dora's first thought was that she might know her, for by all accounts it was someone from the town. A young woman, who worked in the hotel. The men that Dora had seen this morning when she was looking down from the empty bedroom, well – Morality was gasping to get the story out – they had brought the news. The news, Dora's mother would appreciate this point, was already two days old. A woman had been found, naked, with a bag over her head on the waste ground by the tannery. 'The place they make the people park now,' said Morality.

Shot in the head, 'her nipples had been hacked right off!'

Dora was at the sink. The sewing machine was on the table. Lydney was helping her, leant across her to put something on the draining board. Morality was going on with the story.

'It's true, as I stand here it's true. She'd been entertaining PKFs, you know . . . and they got her. They don't know where it was done, not yet, but they stripped her naked and they shot her, then they cut her nipples off. Down at the tannery, someone walking a dog found her, a bag over her head.'

What was Dora doing? 'A bag over her head.'

Lydney stretched across again, this time to move the machine farther down the table, but it was too late for Dora. A trickle of blood ran down her leg.

'Tea?' asked Lydney. 'Chop, chop.'

The story hung low in the air over Carver. For a while at least it divided the women from their men. On Wednesday the fishman was surrounded for the latest news. The sagging bulk of Mrs Pierce in her red shapeless cardigan, knitted out of balls of unravelled wool, her flat hair beneath her flat head scarf. Dora stood and talked to her a while. Dora couldn't stomach Netty, but was discovering that Mrs P of the slipping stockings was of a different type. They weren't friends, far from it, but Mrs P would stand and chat a while, Netty lingered only long enough to judge.

A breeze of nervousness played in the tops of the Scotch pines that afternoon, the fishman saying that whether he was here or not next week rather depended. His, 'What can I do for you ladies this afternoon?' was a bit peremptory.

'You watch. He'll not be making the journey up here much longer. Mark my words,' said Netty, adding for good measure the symbolic act of his forgetting to throw anything out for the dogs.

A shivering in the trees, a sudden nervousness, the women making a space between themselves and their men, the men who, by their silence, condoned such brutal punishment for collaboration.

There were no books about pregnancy at Stephen's place and Dora didn't want to make a fool of herself, didn't want to ask. For some reason she found she couldn't ask about anything these days. She had not asked Stephen what he felt about the hacked woman and he had not said anything to her. The enjoyment of an afternoon out at The Rinkha seemed pathetic now. She felt increasingly anxious, unable to settle to anything at all. She went up to the church with some idea of praying for the unknown woman, though she did not believe in any God. She found the big door locked. There were footprints around the entrance, footprints in the muddy grass and a sense, as in the early days when she had hardly dared to walk into her own kitchen, of something going on here that she was not a party to, something going on.

Lydney, ubiquitous, appeared as she walked back down the short-cut to the house. They had to walk in single file on the narrow path with its overhanging holly branches. It gave Dora the confidence to speak.

'The men who brought the news about the woman, Lydney? Who were those men?'

'Casuals, labourers,' he explained.

Labourers? Unlikely, coming all the way up here.

'Religious, were they?' she asked, not knowing really why she asked it, but Lydney gave her a queer look as they parted at the end of the footpath.

'I don't know what you're on about,' he said, apparently quite baffled, 'I don't know what you mean.'

Dora was not sure what she meant either, though she knew that almost by accident what she said had touched him. The men she'd seen by chance from the empty bedroom window didn't look like casual labourers who walk for miles around the countryside looking for work. There was no casual work on farms in the winter – even she knew that. They had come to Lydney in search of something else. They, or others, had been together recently at the church.

Something seemed to be seeping out of Dora and it wasn't only blood. She had no one to talk to; all of a sudden she felt she'd lost her confidence. She felt anxious and at risk in Carver. It wasn't that they were against her but that she was on her own. Peace hung over the soup plates, the paper fluttered in the draught whenever anyone opened or closed the kitchen door.

Dora steeled herself to mention the hacked woman.

'You don't think it was justified, Stephen?'

'What do you take me for?' he said.

Had Lydney said something about Angelo's. 'Do you think it was justified?' How could she ask him that? He wasn't ready for the answer and that evening, for the second time, he turned away from her in bed.

Dora would get her courage up, bring up the subject of Lydney and the church. It was finding the right moment that was difficult. She forgot that time was short.

The Tribune newspaper showed signs of edginess. Stephen read between the lines of Junior's editorials, then tried, valiantly, to forget what he thought he saw. And Dora, well Dora was waiting for the right moment, waiting for some intimacy that would smooth the path. The right moments these days were few and far between. He was drawing away from her, at least that's what she thought. She lay beside him in their marriage bed, she didn't want to talk. And in the end she did what times of war had taught her: ignored the wreath in the hedge and the writing on the road. She did not give word to her worries, as if giving word to them might make them true. She didn't mention anything to Stephen because above all she felt unsure of his reaction, felt that they hadn't been together long enough, felt that least said was soonest mended, felt blocked – still felt that anything about his parents, about Carver, was in his eyes not her business, sacrosanct. What she feared was the veil that came over her brother's face when she had prodded him, the veil that Lydney wore.

The PFKs continued to drive up each day to collect the milk. They did not come at any other time, and when they came for milk they didn't linger over it, sniff about. They continued to hit the gatepost even though it had been painted white. One morning Dora watched from the scullery, Stephen asking the soldier to be more careful, putting his hand in the stone which they'd knocked off the gatepost as if it were a wound.

'That's the one my mum fancies,' said Morality, her little shadow, 'the little dark one, gorgeous don't you think?'

SEVEN

Early spring brought dank and misty days, the ground chewed up all around The Sevens where Stephen worked with Enda, helped by Ralph and Frankie between shifts. The muffled sounds in the mist: the tap-tap of the weatherboarding going up on either side of the terrace, and the sawing of the wood.

I'm going to live outside history? Dora despised herself for being weak. She considered slipping the church key off Lydney's key-ring but that was ridiculous – he couldn't refuse her if she asked for it. She watched from the scullery as he went into his little office, then walked in after him and came out with the key.

Dora unlocked the church, endowed by the Childes, restored by the Childes, stone hands clasped together. No services since the Feast of the White Saint at the beginning of the occupation. The church smelt faintly of tobacco but was otherwise quite unremarkable, undisturbed. Dora looked hard at the Childe effigy, a woman and a man carved in stone, ancient Childes lying together, his hand on the stone folds of her dress. She stood in the doorway looking out at the graveyard. She tried to see it with Stephen's or with Lydney's eyes, tried to understand. Back inside she ran her finger around the stone bowl of

83

the font – tap, slide, tap, 'You praying that you're pregnant, Dora?'

'No, I'm not.'

'Maggie's pregnant. You ought to talk to her.'

Dora forbore to comment but silence didn't stop Morality, never had.

'Maggie says she can't bear to brush up against anything because of her breasts, they're that tender! And they've grown.' Morality looked at Dora's chest with disappointment. 'I mean, if you're not sick and your breasts don't hurt or anything, you can't be. Mum says it's probably hysterical.'

'You didn't tell your mother, Morality! You promised not to! Now everyone will be laughing at me behind my back. God, Morality!' she cursed her as she relocked the church door. 'Christ!'

'I didn't mean to tell her. It just sort of slipped out. Cross my heart and hope to die.'

'Well that's the last confidence I have with you. Okay?'

'Okay, okay.'

Apparently Maggie was about to chuck The Rinkha, the smell of frying made her sick.

'She can't touch coffee.'

Morality was full of it. Maggie had retched five times in the space of five minutes, paraffin got up her nose. Netty had told Maggie that the sicker she was the firmer the pregnancy. Dora listened with compulsive masochism.

'Freak pregnancy's quite common.' Morality made it sound like getting a puncture on a bike, 'It happens all the time.'

84

Planting went on at Hooley's Field – the ground cleared, each sapling tied to a small white stick. The twins measured the distance between the saplings and were paid for it; Tom Allen grumpily added manure to every hole. Stephen spent hours down there; Dora suspected him of wanting to get out of the house. Even when the trees were all in he couldn't leave it. The plot had to be fenced with rabbit wire, more wire tacked on to a wooden frame as a little makeshift gate. He'd stand there for hours and look at it, look at what he'd done. Dora became jealous of the little trees.

The best part of Stephen's day was walking down there in the lighter evenings, looking at his precious orchard which was only just visible from the house and looked like a distant burial ground, line after line of small white sticks. The weather was fine and bright with a wind that seemed to cut right through one's clothing. Wind tugged at Stephen's saplings but, strapped to their supports, they remained safe and firm. The twins played PKFs these days and had made one of the sculleries their base. Morality mucked about with Dora's sewing machine; miraculously a key bit of it got lost. Maggie had left The Rinkha and languished around at Netty's. Netty, who'd had enough of it, preferred to play midwife to Dora's marmalade, Netty's idea in the first place, already decanted once, now back in the preserving pan because it hadn't set. Happy in the hideous apron, Netty washed out the sticky jars in the sink as Dora, under instruction, took samples of it on a saucer which she balanced on the window sill.

'Yuck. I'll never want to eat this stuff again. It's freezing with this window open.'

Netty was loving all of it, particularly Dora's incompetence. She talked of 'a rolling boil', fussed round Dora, insisted that the jam was made properly.

'It's got to form a skin.'

Lydney came in, Stephen followed, pockets bulging with tapes and nails and slide rules, just as Morality went tap, slide, tap, so Stephen now jingle-jangled. He threw himself, his coat still on, into the nearest chair. He'd hit his thumb with a hammer; he sucked it.

'Bests has gone.' Lydney laid the newspaper out on the table between the jam pots.

'It never has!' said Netty.

They gathered round the paper, 'Look at that!'

Dora read over Lydney's shoulder: the smell of aftershave. Bests department store had been burnt to the ground, killing two auditors working there over the weekend.

'Selling stuff to those it shouldn't have,' said Netty smugly, for Bests, like most of the other shops, had been trading with the troops. Bests, 'Biggest in the West', whose fortunes had begun humbly enough with the invention of felt and hare-skin chest warmers in the days of the dinosaurs; Bests which had grown from a single shop to spread itself from the High Street right around the corner and made it Bests' Corner – gone. Bests where Dora had bought her wedding dress; Bests' catalogue that hung on a nail in The Rinkha – gone. Marmalade reaching setting point and well beyond.

Two dead at Bests, and over the page news that

the dentist had been shot. Shot in his own surgery, fallen in a last gesture of defiance, protecting his fish tanks. Had he been filling soldiers' teeth? Dora remembered the door of the dentist's, the house with the delicate fanlight she'd so hated. The house always approached with dread, even her mother weakening, arriving for an appointment then telling the maid that she had actually only come to say she had to change it. The surgery curtains that Dora had concentrated on so miserably as a child during her sessions in the chair, the smell of gas.

'Hotting up,' said Netty warmly.

'This is only the beginning.' Was it Lydney or Stephen who said that?

'Peace is a ball you can toss high in the air.'

Dora would like to take Junior the poet to one side. Peace. Gone were the days when Stephen lay in bed beside her and discussed it; peace is a ball that lies between you that neither dare pick up? Instinct had made her wary of his wilder plans, but now she longed for him to talk like that again. To talk of the future with confidence, our children and our children's children; since the news of the hacked woman he hadn't talked like that. And winter went on forever here, she felt so isolated, she never heard from anyone, she might as well be dead. April was colder than March and now, just when the wind dropped enough for Stephen to start rethatching, he was summoned to present himself at the PKF head-quarters in the town.

Dora was cross with herself and cross with him, as cross and frustrated as when she was a child trying to move something heavy out of her path. Carver was the block, love was the block, why couldn't she be strong?

The morning was cold of course, hoar frost covering the weatherboarding, bogged ground once more iced over, hens pecking in the yard where Netty had thrown out the scraps.

She was cross with herself, cross with Stephen, so why did she kiss him in the doorway, then at the van, then get into the van and kiss him several times again? He was wearing what would forever after be his wedding coat, she pulled the collar up around his neck. There was so much she ought to say to him, now not later. 'Keep warm.' She kissed him thoroughly again.

EIGHT

Soldiers manned the bridges into town. Stephen was directed to park behind the tannery and walk in. Troops dressed in blue and khaki took his papers, questioned him, delayed his progress. Others lounged across the parapet of the bridge, a child's hat blew off in the wind, landing on and sinking into brown lake water. Stephen was jostled on the bridge by the soldiers, stared at, questioned and questioned again; the smell of the tannery from across the water was mixed now with smells of fire. A sense of hurry in the town, soldiers all over the place, windows boarded, the shutters up at Blakes and at the other bars.

Stephen put his head in at the post office, meaning to complain, but the room was full of people with the same idea. He waited his turn in a large and buzzing queue until the postmaster came out and stood on a box to address them all. No, he couldn't say when regular services would be resumed. Restrictions on transport, all complaints to be directed to the PKF. Some of the crowd were shouting now; Stephen extricated himself from them, went on. Past burnt out Bests and to the hotel which had been fortified with scaffolding and wire. He showed his summons and was directed in.

He knew them all. The hill farmers, rather rakish looking in their town clothes, closed and unforgiving faces that did not forget. Willie was up from Gobbins – they might have travelled together if he'd known. Willie with his son, the Bonbon, Midway's hope and Stephen's childhood hero. The Bonbon, middle-aged now, who had been knocked senseless in a boxing bout as a teenager, went everywhere with his father, unable to look out for himself. The head of mart was there and Stephen's Aunt Florida, the only woman present, the perm she'd had to celebrate her presidency of the Farmer's Co-operative Dairy already growing out. Meades, the owner of the tannery, and Junior Hall, the editor of *The Tribune*; Stephen was the last to arrive and Florida was talking to Meades. He failed to catch her eye.

He stood on his own by the window with his back to them, his hands in his pockets. Compromise? Lydney didn't see it quite that way. 'Supping with the enemy' summed up his feelings about a meeting with the PKF. Stephen looked out of the window, his attention caught by an argument in the street below, between a butcher, a van driver unloading carcasses and a rough old lorry laden with coal bricks, its driver leaning out of the cab and shouting, insisting on turning right. The driver flung himself down from the cab, leaving the door wide open, and went at the butcher like a bull.

'Gentlemen, ladies, shall we make a start?'

Why were they all here, what would they get out of it? Stephen, torn away from the window, was ushered to sit down, found the only seat available, next to the army officer on the curve of the old oval table. The oval table around which Bests had held their annual staff dinners, toasted the haberdashery department, which, in a difficult year, could be congratulated – again.

Everyone else was smoking, Stephen too lit up; Stephen, a bit exposed by his place at the table, but at least in this position close to the two-inch map which, as his glance fell on it, was whipped away, suspended on the back of the door. Stephen discovered that by edging his chair as close to the officer as possible he could avoid his gaze: the lighthouse beam, sweeping down and across the table.

He caught his aunt's eye, one of her looks. Be serious? Take care? Coffee and biscuits were provided straight away, Stephen was surprised to find his hands were shaking, shook so much that he decided against milk; it was their milk anyway. He thought of the crunch as the PKF truck hit the wall; their milk, and rumour had it that what the PKFs took was always watered down.

The officer introduced himself as Captain Dalmar, and opened the proceedings by detailing the extent of their forces, where they were billeted, 'what you already know'.

'What you're prepared to tell us,' said Junior Hall.

Dalmar's smile had the strength of summer sun in it. A previous meeting with Junior had, he felt, established a working rapport, their differences already taking on a safe and ritual note.

The meeting had been called in response to the present state of unrest, a delicate way of putting it, windows boarded, shops burnt down, dentists shot. Would there be heckling from the back? Would some-one shout, 'We've got you rattled'? Would anybody dare?

The captain spoke of obligations and responsi-bilities, of co-operation and mutual dependence, of the desirability of an end to commercial disruption, of the link between business and security, easing himself gently into his notes. Notes which, though part of them might prove unpopular, made good sense – wonderful notes, notes that he was proud of. Notes devised with a built-in space for underlining this point and explaining that. Notes which could only be deliv-ered by him; notes which gave the impression that he was more than willing, in this summoned com-pany, to deviate a little, to address them off the cuff, had been carefully contrived. Dalmar, at the head of the table, working them, an old dog running a new flock.

The Allegiance Act was read again, explained again, enlarged upon. Dalmar driving them along the hedge, through the gap, down hill, down hill.

'Why is a curfew necessary?'

Here we go.

The night Dalmar described was of the darkest and most hellish sort, moonless, without stars. He was talking of the night that endangered his troops. 'Under cover of darkness.' Stephen placed in that night the memory of the dentist and his fish, before remembering that the dentist had been shot while removing his instruments from the sterilising jar, the dentist had been shot in the morning.

The curfew came into force from tomorrow; the

penalty for breaking it was death. Stephen wondered whether the dentist had been buried yet, whether those who'd previously missed appointments had turned up?

Why had they been summoned, what were they all doing here? Surely there was nothing to discuss? They were being told, not even persuaded, that these were the new rules. On went Dalmar, down hill, down hill, anticipating some fancy footwork at the ford; spring rains, the river running fast and deep, 'How will my safety be protected and those of my loved ones?'

Ah, here was the nub. Information. Nothing was too small to pass on, they would be the ones to decide what was trivial and what was worthy of being followed up. 'Make contact with us.' In it together. Divide and conquer was the gist. Stephen shifted his chair as unobtrusively as possible back to its original position. At close range, Dalmar's smiles were as routine as punctuation marks. Each time he smiled, the Bonbon gave a big smile back.

'What do I mean by unusual circumstances?' or to put it in plain words, 'On whom should I inform?' Absenteeism, strange comings and goings, the car in the lay-by, unknowns seen in your area, strangers on the move. The desirability – this word for the second time – of an organised network of informants.

'Whom can you trust? You can't trust anyone.' The enemy of peace is the man you know, the friend you went to school with, your neighbour, possibly – tweaking a rubber band in his fingers – a member of your own family. 'This is cowboy country,' Dalmar said, quoting one of Junior's editorials, making a mistake for what people say about themselves is one thing, what a stranger says quite another.

Without raising his head to look at the others, Stephen felt the atmosphere deteriorating.

His aunt, who had for some time been grinding her cigarettes brutally into the ashtray, confronted Dalmar about gas supplies. Only Dalmar was surprised. This rather masculine, stubby woman, her make-up – 'You really need something nearer your skin tone Miss Childe' – like warpaint, the shoulders that could heft a creamery can with the best of them.

'Captain Dalmar, I really must insist.'

Off she went. Everyone knew and trusted Florida. Quite effortlessly she defused the atmosphere, for no one was going to inform the PKF of anything, that was fairly clear. Did Dalmar know this, did he take it in? Did he realise what Florida was up to? Florida, veteran of the committee room, an old hand at what she would call successfully pulling the wool. So the meeting would unite on gas supplies or the lack of them. They rallied behind Florida; even Meades, known as a bit of a eunuch, now took heart.

'We must pass on, I'm afraid. Further questions at the end of the meeting.'

Hang on there, they weren't having that! For they'd been through the millrace already for these people. How many of them, only this morning, had been stopped, questioned, searched? In their town, in their country, in the name of peace. Interference in ordinary private lives became the war cry, and Junior had a word for it: 'privation'.

'First a curfew, then restrictions on basic facilities. Light and heat . . .'

'Condemned to darkness,' Meades proclaimed quite bravely, for like the others he preferred the trouble he was used to, baulked when it came to this rigid, imposed peace.

Junior made a note for his newspaper, 'Privation in the western region, peace-keepers offer all night and no day.'

Dalmar's notes written for reasonable people. This too was a mistake. He had allowed time, but he hadn't allowed enough time; he went through gas supplies again. And still the meeting wasn't satisfied. Meades asked for it to be put on record, his disapproval of the way things were now being run.

'Or not run!'

A farmer spoke now, his voice wobbly with nerves. He wanted to make a small point but a point worth mentioning. His voice cracked at his own daring, as he spoke of wastage by the very people who now asked them to make sacrifices, to cut down.

'There are two gas heaters going in this room.'

'And far too many lights on.' The Bonbon looked up at the lights.

Meades now complained of high-handedness, all parking moved to the tannery without a word to him . . .

'Security regulations have already been discussed,' Dalmar reminded him.

'Discussed!' Meades spat the word into the room.

And Florida could have argued on forever about the position of the hill farms, what he called cowboy country. Well, the cowboys were finding their lives pretty thin – outlying farms, needless drudgery. The

PKF would have to look after the farmers better if the farmers were to continue to look after them.

'Food and milk.'

'Road blocks, security checkpoints, hold-ups.'

'If transportation is in your hands now,' Junior cut in, 'if security is indeed so linked to commerce, surely it should now be more efficient rather than less?'

'May we move on to worship?' Dalmar said against a buzz of talk.

Worship. From now on Father Cuffe would take charge of all western parishes, and could be contacted through this hotel. It was hoped that regular services would soon be resumed. In the interim, and under the Allegiance Act, the churches were to be kept locked.

'Printed material. It is now an offence to . . .'

Dalmar continued with his notes but no one listened. Against all his instincts, the officer raised his voice. Junior scribbled shorthand in his notebook, pages of newsprint occurred to him, so much more exciting than a poem. 'Less like peace-keeping, more like siege. Take-over by peace-keepers. Peace-keepers keep us in the dark, curfew imposed, prisoners in our own homes . . .'

Meades opened the window, making a very pointed remark about fresh air, and still it went on, sentences beginning, 'In the event of . . .'

Stephen had long since ceased to write anything down. His place at the table cut him off from the rest, but the real distance was mental rather than physical for Stephen felt no outrage, only fear. The west would resist this peace, just as they'd resisted earlier peace moves far less heavy-handedly imposed.

'You feel as if your generation has been singled out to start again.' He looked across at Junior Hall, those words could have another meaning.

In this crowded room he felt isolated, in this warm room he felt cold, in this well-lit room Stephen felt a premonition of darkness, black as the water underground.

'Your friend, the man you went to school with.' Nat Lydney, Ralph and Frankie, Enda Frere? The hiss of the disputed gas fires; Florida lighting a cigarette with her hands cupped as if she was in the centre of a field; thoughts filled with Dora; the tally one made in the margin – got this, lost that. Stephen turned his paper sideways, drew the butcher, the coal man and the lorry driver, all at loggerheads.

'And may I take this opportunity to wish you . . .' Stephen got up. The air was stifling, but he couldn't leave the room. One by one the men came up to him, to make sure of him, to shake him by the hand. His hand worked but his voice didn't, he couldn't lift his voice up, he felt no outrage only dread. At last he left with Florida, stood with her on the steps of the hotel as she waited for her neighbour, one of the easterners who'd bought property, years ago, on the far side of the lake. She was giving him a lift, she looked tired, she hated waiting, she was anxious to get off.

He wanted to congratulate her for what she'd done there in the meeting, yet he hated her for it as well. The others knew where they stood, because that's where they'd always stood, but Stephen had wanted, so desperately, to move forward now, to stand somewhere else. And she didn't question his politics, why

97

should she? Like Lydney, she would have been astonished at the change.

'You'll never believe it,' she said, as they watched her neighbour cross the road towards them. 'We must be in a crisis. He told me his age the other day, sixty-six, he doesn't look it does he?' She already had her car keys in her fingers, 'Off we go.' Stephen took her arm for a moment, held her back. He wanted to keep hold of her for just a little longer though there was absolutely nothing he could say,

'I don't know how you smoke those things,' she said tapping her own packet after he had offered her his cigarettes. 'If you're stuck,' she whispered in his ear as Dalmar passed between them, 'I know Reenie's got all sorts stashed away.'

'I hope we meet again under happier circumstances.' The well-preserved neighbour shook his hand. Stephen stood for a moment before walking to his own car. He did not see either of them again.

NINE

Pam Jukes was naturally cheerful and pretty in the provocative way that Morality had inherited, though she didn't look too good this morning and she found it more difficult than usual to see the funny side of anything at all.

Morality was doing her hair. Pam wanted some colour in it, and the cottage stank of peroxide as Morality went to work on her with a hint of honey over the kitchen sink.

'Go easy,' Pam warned as Morality tweaked the bits of hair between the fine holes of a rubber cap, 'and I don't want big chunks remember. I don't want to come out looking like a badger.'

'Shut up and let me do it then. I promise it'll be fine.'

'Every relationship between men and women is simply a transaction,' Lydney had said to Pam. What an impoverished little man: the wintry voice he used for such pronouncements, insisting she accept the value he put on it. They were both adults, he played a lot on that. What happened between them was a transaction, an exchange; as if it was an adult thing to belittle love. Morality must never know what Pam's affair with Lydney had cost her, Morality had to be preserved from that.

'You used to spend the night.'

'I was pleasuring myself.'

Well, Pam was pleasuring herself now. She had a new admirer, she wouldn't cough the heart out of her chest for the likes of Nat. Nat . . . Pam sat staring at the empty grate, the ridiculous rubber cap on, no make-up. The affair with Lydney had become both clinical and sordid, adult, yes if adult meant it was something one did not tell one's children. Adult because there were things one could never tell. Things that one put up with, stomached, things of which one felt ashamed. Things that Pam wanted to protect her daughter from. 'You can't love to order.' Mrs Pierce had told her that. Love. Transaction. Well, Pam was paying Morality with the money Lydney had left for her, this was a transaction. She had thought of taking Maggie's job on at The Rinkha, but honestly, after what she'd been through, why strain herself, why bother?

'This better be good,' she told her daughter.

'It'll be brilliant, Mum.'

Now the green road was truly green. Spring. The alarm calls of blackbirds with a cat lying still beneath the nest. The frantic baaing as the ewes and lambs are let out together and bleat until they find each other in the field. Rams pensioned off beneath the plum trees with the hens. Spring. No strength in the sun yet, but a warmth in the breeze. A high note sounding somewhere for those like Netty Frere who cared to listen. A sense of suspension, a warning, a thin note, a high note held before the music breaks.

Stephen had not said much about the PKF meeting, but then Dora hadn't asked. Ignore the wreath in the hedge and hope it goes away?

Warmer weather and the caravan of the house moving itself outside, Dora thinking, as the days went past, that tomorrow she would sort a few things out with Stephen. But what exactly was she going to say? Some assurance that if there was trouble he wouldn't have a part in it, that he'd stick by peace, by her, and not by Carver Hill. It was quite ridiculous yet it seemed such a delicate question to put to him. 'I am where I come from,' she remembered that.

He had started to draw again: now his pockets bulged more than ever – nails, screws, bradawl, tape, spirit level, soft pencil and pad. When he drew, absorption wiped from his face the expression she'd got used to, his defensive, anxious look. A happy concentration on his face when he drew, the look she remembered from when she knew him as a child. On it went. Whatever they filled their days with it wasn't talk; on it went, not saying what she should say, hoping that the crisis, still only imagined, might slip past.

If you can't beat them, join them. On fine evenings she walked with Stephen down to Hooley's Field, mooned with him over his budding trees. How little she'd known at the beginning; did every married couple live like this? Moving round, beside, above the things that hung between them, limbo dancing underneath the pole. Marriage was as delicate as the game of spillikins, a balancing act, a growing list of things they couldn't broach. Quite easy in each other's company but not open, not truthful; walking together, chatting but not sharing anything that really mattered.

Now it was Stephen who extricated himself from the bedclothes, Stephen who couldn't sleep. Maggie's baby wasn't his, this was a blessing from a sympathetic god. It had occurred to him, and to the rest of Carver, but then you see not everyone gets caught. Boy, did he hang on to that. The payments to Lydney continued but he had not asked yet for anything else, no fireworks, no explosion. Stephen waited for something to happen. Nothing did. Sitting it out was an agony though. One moment he felt his fate was a foregone conclusion, the next he thought his mind had run away with him, he had hope. Vacillating between stasis and panic, horror and hope, he drew to keep his mind occupied. Not drawing, he was caught in a paralysis of fear.

Lydney would suck him in, set up something; he was probably fixing it right now. Lydney would tell Dora about Angelo's, if he hadn't told her already. He would tell her about Maggie Frere. Stephen tried to read the signs in Dora – he imagined her being frightened by him, appalled by him, disgusted by him. What she didn't know couldn't hurt her. On the contrary, it hurt him. Could he keep out of it, this time? Would Lydney, for old times' sake, allow him a little grace? Could he continue to live at Carver and turn a blind eye to what he suspected might be going on? Or was it all just a mix of guilt and imagination, the product of getting away with everything for so long?

Stephen couldn't settle to anything. He glanced through the newspapers, drank a lot of coffee, avoided Lydney as much as possible, avoided situations with Dora that might end in tricky talk. He sat on his chair beneath the angel ceiling looking out.

The twins had started using the garden as a place to play. The monkey puzzle tree, planted by his grandfather, seemed to draw them – an old and threadbare creature it was now, with its strange tassels at the top, its bark peeling off like coconut. At weekends, kids from Midway joined them, used the monkey puzzle as a sort of base. Games hadn't changed much since he was a child, although playing at soldiers was something he'd never done. The game enacted before him this spring morning was familiar. One child stood at the base of the tree, another kicked a can as a signal for the others to run off. The child by the tree remained on watch, he had to seek the other children but not allow them to get back to the tree and touch it. The kids had made paths through the long grass. He looked at the flattened bits where the children ran, he looked at the monkey puzzle. He had to look away.

Sometimes, these days, when he was drawing he simply had to stop, to leave off in the middle, to cut out. Closing one eye to the facts around him had strained the other eye, he could only see how temporary it all was. He imagined the tree cut down and lying out across the grass, indenting the grass. A moment's panic and a feeling that he couldn't breathe, panic. What is a moment? A sort of joke time, how long does it last? He paced the long gallery to calm himself until the moment passed.

Looking down into the empty garden at the grass, he could see the pattern of the children's game, how it had ended in a wrestling match, like games he'd had with Ralph and Frankie, Nat. Games that ended when one of them sneaked up. The ghost of himself in the long grass, playing, putting out his hands to save himself, falling backwards into the grass. He remembered the feel of falling, catching his head on a stone, yelling out blue murder. Falling backwards into the soft grass, playing dead until he was tickled into standing up.

He wanted to run to Dora, put his head in her lap; 'This is what I am. Do you still love me? I've done some things, I may be asked to do some others.'

Jesus Christ, he even had to use euphemisms when talking to himself! Carver. Morality and the twins and Maggie and Netty, Netty shouting 'Tea!' and the smell of frying and children coming running. Enda shaking the sawdust from the folds of his trousers. Morality and the twins, and Maggie and Netty, Mrs Pierce, Dora, falling backwards into the soft grass of the garden; he imagined them all dead. Silence where once there was noise, cold ash 'where once there had been fire, a door banging shut in the wind.

'You did it Stephen. You brought it all down on our heads.'

The tree was down and he hid the axe where they would never find it, but they saw the tree and they found the axe.

'You did it Stephen. Trying to move the mountain, to make the river run up hill.'

TEN

Ralph Pierce and his brother were moonlighting, the weather seemed set fair. Ralph thatching the ridge up on The Sevens, new straw on Amy Lind's round white stones. Dora behaving like her mother in a crisis, ignoring wreaths and ironing shirts. Frankie brought some thatch over and filled the dip of the open cattle shed in the yard where the calves were over-wintered. He was a neat worker and he finished what he began. In no time at all he had pinned the thatch in and covered it with chicken wire.

For a spell, almost two weeks, the end of May and into June, the weather was baking hot. In the shade of the long eaves cast by the new thatch Netty sewed, shooing the fowls that she'd pluck later, which now pecked and dust-bathed around her feet. Maggie, legs apart already, peeled spuds into a bucket, nicking out the eyes. Mrs Pierce simply sat, hands idle in her lap, a man's hat on her head.

A stillness in the heat, the chorus of women who neither cut Dora out of their conversations nor truly cut her in. Netty holding the needle away from her face, 'Do this for me, pet, I can't see for looking.' Maggie wiping her wet hands on her skirt. Dora watching. To be asked to thread a needle!

Heat. Lulls in the conversation which started and stopped again, shunted, went a little further on.

Maggie expected her baby in November. Dora tried to imagine November and completely failed. Father Cuffe now lodged at Stephen's place on and off, snored outside with his feet on an upturned basket, sleeping off his lunch. He cleaved to the women but sat up smartly enough at the sight or sound of Lydney. In the company of the men of Carver he would, if at all possible, attach himself to Dora, engaging her without preamble in a long conversation, talking nineteen to the dozen as if his life depended on it, until the men had gone. Once or twice Dora had been on the point of stopping this charade, of asking him what he was frightened of, but she didn't want to know the answer, decided not.

Dora Parks, who would recognise her now? Here, on hot summer afternoons, half-listening to the women talk, modestly subdued. Stories of the marriages, births and deaths of Carver and Midway. Ectopic pregnancies and diabetes, sciatica, septicaemia. Faults, like a seam in the earth, that ran right through families; Tom Allen's short-lived marriage to Pam Jukes.

'Some say he couldn't do it.'

'He frightened her to death.'

'It's the quiet ones you have to worry over, mark my words.'

'I'd like a quiet one then,' said Morality, not knowing that it was a conversation about her father with which she now joined in.

'He wrote a poem about it.' Netty whispered,

nudging Mrs Pierce. 'He sent it to her, I seen it, years ago when she first come back from Starveall.'

'Mum reckons it'll come to a head soon.' Morality, not to be ignored.

'Fine lot she knows.'

'My mum says the PKF are starting cracking down.'

'Where'd she get that from then?'

'She got it from the little birdies, didn't she?' Maggie winking at the others. Pam was up to her old tricks again, this time with a PKF.

Netty gave her daughter a pointed look.

'Those for dinner. You best get on with it.'

Maggie, one cross word started her off these days, tears . . .

'Now look what you done,' chimed Morality.

'You got a mouth on you an' all.'

'I have not.'

Lydney, shirt sleeves uniformly rolled, took a drink from a cup by the pump several yards away. The older women dropped their voices, Morality raised hers, 'My mum says what happens here is down to Ranelagh.'

'Who's he when he's at home then?' Maggie sniggered.

'Leave her be,' warned Netty.

'He's . . .'

'You don't know your arse from your elbow, child,' said Mrs Pierce, deciding things had gone quite far enough. 'Now give us all a bit of peace or run along.' She leant down and threw a stick at the chickens. 'You can get along an' all. And don't get into a snot on me, Miss Morality,' she said giving her

Maggie's bucket of potatoes, 'you hang around out here, you got to help.'

'If anyone touches the PKFs, they'll come and kill us in our beds.' Morality, high heels almost tripping her, crossed the yard with the beastly bucket, smiling at Lydney, hoping that he'd heard.

Dora was playing with the kittens when the Bonbon arrived like an apparition in the yard. She thought for a moment he was going to tread on the kittens: the big, lumbering creature, dressed only in a night-shirt and boots, coming towards her with a dazed expression as if he wasn't going to stop. She put her hand out to his chest and the touch of her hand stopped him. He turned and leant with his back against the yard wall, screwed his eyes up at the sun for a moment and then slid down the wall, with not a word spoken, until he was sitting on his hunkers there, looking at the ground.

Netty got some sense out of him; the PKFs had come for his father, had taken him away. The Bonbon had fed the stock at Gobbins but not himself. He had come wandering across the hillside in his night things, hungry and dirty but otherwise unharmed.

For once Dora was glad of Netty's assistance. The two women fed him in the kitchen. Dora fetched him some of Stephen's things, but the effort of changing proved too much for him. He sat on the kitchen bench at the table, his big head almost in his soup plate, crying. Crying, a big man like that, even Netty was upset. Morality put her head around the door but went again when Dora put her fingers to her lips. Dora stroked the Bonbon's tangled hair. Netty moved the soup plate out of harm's way and replaced it with a cushion, talked to him in a lullaby voice, holding one of those enormous, dirty hands.

Leaving him with Netty, Dora and Morality walked across to Gobbins hardly speaking for the sadness and the heat. The farm, when they reached it, was a tiny stone place known locally as the sugar lump. Not much more than a series of sagging leantos, fresh cow pats among the pots and pans, bedding, chairs, that had been thrown outside.

'I said the PKFs were going to crack down,' crowed Morality, though even she was slightly awed, 'looking for guns most like.'

'Every farmer has a gun, Morality.' Yet it was of course quite possible despite the old man's age. A small place like this in the middle of nowhere.

They sat down in the mess on the rough grass. Morality kept picking stuff up, going through it, making comments, private property public on the grass.

'Leave it alone, Morality.'

'Only looking!'

'Don't take anything.'

'Okay!'

Dora was at a loss what to do – silence, just the buzz in the long grasses.

'Do you think he . . . ?'

'What, Morality?'

'You know . . .' Morality had that look on her face.

Dora guessed what she was talking about for the Bonbon was the cause of all sorts of local speculation.

'You know . . .' Morality said again. 'Do you think he does it . . . ?'

'I know what you're getting at and I've no idea.'

'He's like a great big bear . . .'

'Oh, for goodness sake!'

'There's no reason why he shouldn't be able to . . .'

Dora got up and walked away rather than hit her, went into the house.

Morality followed. 'Shall we tidy it?' she asked.

'Do shut up!'

The door was off its hinges, everything inside the two-roomed house was smashed or broken – crockery, the globes of oil lights, the leg of the stool, more bedclothes trailed halfway down the stairs.

'God,' said Dora hopelessly.

'They're probably just putting the frighteners on.' Another phrase Morality had overheard.

'He can't stay here now, can he?' Dora was really talking to herself. He couldn't manage on his own. Why couldn't the PKFs just have taken his father, without breaking up the farm. She picked up some coloured glass from the floor and put it on a window sill. 'Look at all this mess!'

'They set fire to some places.'

'I'm sure they don't.'

'They come in the night and set fire to places. The Bonbon must have nearly shit himself.'

'Okay, Morality, okay!'

They brought in the stuff from outside, Morality swept glass into a corner, Dora took a pair of boots and the clothes that were lying on the iron bed upstairs. Father and son in the same bed, a candlestick on the deep, recessed window that looked out across the hill. It'll kill him, she thought. Bastards. Dora pulled the thin and dirty curtains across the two downstairs windows and then, more to prevent further violation than in obeisance to Special Powers, she and Morality spent a hot half-hour nailing boards across the broken door.

'Try saying bastards as you hammer,' she suggested, doing it any old how but eventually getting it done.

'What about the cow?' asked Morality.

'What about it?' A cow and following calf looked curiously at them from farther up the track. 'I can't do anything with cows, Morality. I don't know anything about them.'

'Shouldn't we take it back with us?'

'Don't be ridiculous.'

The cow looked at Dora with reproachful eyes as she loaded Morality up with clothes and pushed her on in front of her.

'You're frightened of cows, aren't you?'

'I certainly am not,' claimed Dora walking fast in the opposite direction. 'It's got grass and everything. It'll be fine.'

'She'll be fine.'

'She then.' Dora shoved Morality on in front of her. 'Someone else can cope.'

It was hard to credit, but it was a fact: the Bonbon's father, Archie Meades from the tannery and Dick Joyce, a seventeen-year-old from Mantles Lane in town, were charged with the arson attack on Bests. The Bonbon showed no emotion after the first tears at the table, went willingly, almost eagerly, when the PKFs took him to the hospital in the town.

'Docile, that one,' commented Morality. It was what Netty had said.

Tom Allen went up to Gobbins once a day to check the animals, reboarded the door. Mice crept into the empty house, small feet tripping around its broken contents. The PKF stepped up surveillance round Midway, New Mills and Carver. Suspicion hung over this tiny corner like a cloud.

News of the arrests was greeted with elaborate disbelief. *The Tribune* was full of it. Dick Joyce's mother filled the press with poems and photographs to touch the strongest heart. She was interviewed and willing to give the contents of her breakfast if it would help. Joyce's girlfriend quickly became his fiancée, adding fuel to the fire. Pictures of the trio – mother, girlfriend, son – were spread across the front pages of the paper. Someone wrote a song about them, an appeal was started to raise funds. New life was breathed into the Bonbon's story: 'Knocked senseless at fourteen. Midway boxing bruiser hits the ropes'. Captain Dalmar took some leave that was due to him. *The Tribune* sold more copies than ever before in its long history as Junior went into overdrive.

The weather broke for a week of wind and rain that sent the lilac blossom flying. The ridge of The Sevens was completed and the weatherboarding all but finished, and still Stephen waited for the ultimatum that didn't come.

Dora gave him a hand to whitewash the insides of the two renovated cottages, putting in more hard work than he did. A sort of lassitude had come over him which she tried to put down to the break in the good weather, or the heat of the sun that had preceded it, or something in the water, on the wind . . . With a small brush Stephen drew cartoons for Dora on the bare uneven walls.

'Angels?'

'Not up to angels.'

'You could, you know. I'm sure you could.'

'Don't patronise me, Dora.' That hit home.

The child who'd copied table mats in Mill Street now drew a series of cartoons. She came and sat on his lap on a kitchen chair brought in for her to reach the high bits, she stroked his hair which had paint in it.

'Going grey?'

They were strangers, weren't they? She touched him but she didn't reach him. She didn't even know whether she wanted to reach him any more. He was always preoccupied, he didn't want to talk, she turned to him in bed but he didn't seem to want her now.

'When I went away before . . .'

Were they at last coming to it? Dora stroked the hair she loved, and the back of his brown neck.

'When I went away before, it was because I was ill.'

Ill! Pathetic! What did he take her for, an idiot? A babe new born?

She forced herself to stroke his hair. What was she doing with this man?

'What are you saying, Stephen?' She loved his hair, but she couldn't trust the mouth that spoke to her, the hair was dear to her, the mouth . . .

'Don't lie to me, Stephen.'

'Don't ask questions then.'

She hadn't asked, he had begun to tell her. Did she want to know?

'If you don't tell me Stephen I can't help you.'

'What makes you think I need your help?'

'Stephen.' She hated every part of him; every memory of every intimacy she would strike out. She continued to stroke his hair, the back of his neck.

'What is it?'

Another long pause, 'It's nothing.'

'It's obviously something.'

He moved her off his lap quite tenderly.

'Stephen?'

'Just going to get some air.'

Stephen made a series of very small drawings all in the same pad. He drew the yard gate that Dora had looked so long at in her first weeks in Carver, he drew the monkey puzzle tree. He drew the view from the room with the angel ceiling and copied part of the ceiling itself. He drew Carver from the field barn and his plantation down at Hooley's Field. He drew until the light faded and still he wouldn't come to bed.

ELEVEN

They were working on the third cottage when it happened. Lydney and Stephen stood sideways on to each other in the narrow doorway, the darkness of the interior beyond them. Stephen felt that he couldn't breathe properly, that his lungs had gone shallow, that he had to gasp for air.

Lydney explained the situation, even offered him a guided tour. Guns had been buried down at The Bottoms for a while now, their presence marked with pea sticks for all to see. The churchyard and the church was the meeting place; the so-called casual labourers who appeared periodically in Carver were part of the operation of which Lydney, the Pierces, Enda Frere, but not Tom Allen, were a part. The man who'd killed the dentist came from New Mills, he had lain up in the Field Barn until it was safe to move him on. And now they had a job to do which had nothing to do with renovating cottages. Lydney and the others, well everybody – like those sepia pictures of whole settlements getting the hay in, pulling up the seine net, working on a roof – expected him to lend a hand.

Stephen said nothing.

'You're either with us or against us,' Lydney said.

Very neat.

Ralph and Frankie were in the front room of the cottage, hardly ten yards away. Ralph was plastering, Frankie watched.

'How's it going, do you think?' Frankie whispering, putting his thumb under his cigarette tin to roll one. Ralph caressing the old wall with new plaster, spots of plaster on his trousers and his working boots.

'Hard to tell.'

No raised voices, Stephen and Lydney in the half darkness of the cottage doorway. Lydney spry, Stephen fiddling with the latch he had been about to straighten out.

Why mend anything? Why bother? But he still had a hammer in his hand, he had only to raise the hammer . . . It didn't end there though, did it? Ralph and Frankie, Enda Frere . . .

'A PKF.' Lydney told him, with a gesture towards Pam Jukes's cottage, 'in the next few days. Nothing to it. We – '

'We?'

Lydney took in the Pierces and Carver, Starveall, Gobbins, Midway, New Mills, as far as a little eye can see . . .

'And what if I say "no"?'

'That's another story,' Lydney said.

Stephen walked the green road to the church. He hunched his shoulders as if warding off actual blows, though no blows had fallen. Pity. You get pity only if you've been beaten up. He'd thought he'd feel relief when it came to it, it was only a matter of time, the when or where of it, but he'd thought he'd feel relief.

Exhaustion was what he felt, sheer exhaustion. The urge to lie down on the ground he walked on, the longing to just lie down, roll himself into the ditch, the urge – Dora would say, to prostrate himself – was immense.

They were going to take out Ranelagh. Lydney had it planned. Stephen would take the shot, that way they'd be sure of him. They'd take the body down to Midway to the old quarry now used as the local dump. His men at the cement works would cover up the evidence. Pam wouldn't utter, she knew what happened to collaborators, she wouldn't dare.

Cock of the walk now, Lydney whistled round to visit Pam. He still enjoyed a session with her, his terms, his conditions. He put a bit aside each week to pay for Pam, each coin and each note to tell her what she was worth to him, what she had become. Being with the likes of Pam – as if that was all a man like him had title to expect? She knew what he was on about, he made sure she did. How Lydney dressed now was different. 'Aping your betters?' she'd taunted him, 'mind on higher things?'

'You're Dora,' he said these days when he had sex with her, 'My darling Dora. Dora,' he said as he touched Pam's body, 'Dora doesn't open her legs for just anyone.'

'Dora,' he whispered into her ear lobe, 'Dora.' He knew that hurt.

It hurt, but she could take it now that she had Ranelagh. Let Lydney have his little games, she could handle that. And she wasn't averse to having two lovers, not at all, for her it was a turn-up for the books. She liked to lie in bed of a morning and fantasise about the two of them. They could fight over her if they wanted. She made a point of mentioning one man to the other; she wanted one of them to mind.

She smartened the place up for Ranelagh, Morality noticed that. Ranelagh was younger than she was and he was frightened. He wanted comfort, he wasn't good in bed like Lydney was, he had to feel calm and safe, had to have things nice. He said he was in love with her, it made a change. So it hadn't been a bad spring for Pam all things considered, she got a kick out of having two of them, for the first time in a long time she had fun. Having one just before the arrival of the other, expecting Ranelagh, having Lydney in her back kitchen standing up. She wasn't getting any younger, life owed her a good time.

On that evening she was expecting both of them. She tidied up her little sitting room, she was ever so much more domesticated than people thought. Like Morality, she too had a lot of stuff that came from Stephen's place: two special glasses, run your finger round the outside, engraved. Her standard of living had gone up with Lydney and Ranelagh, though she remembered the hard times when Morality was a baby and she couldn't afford to get drinks in. She usually had a couple of drinks with company expected, 'Dutch courage' drunk from Alice's glasses as she waited on her own. She had a Chinese house-coat, shantung silk it was, you had to iron it damp, and when you ironed it, it smelt a bit beneath the arms. She planned to wear it that evening over a pair of slacks. She had it on the board in front of her when the knock came at the door.

'Bugger.'

It was all nice and settled with Morality up at Dora's and some sandwiches for afterwards already cut. She put the half-ironed housecoat on and quickly dismantled the board, scraping her hand as she put it back into the cupboard beneath the stairs. There was someone behind her, her ex-husband Tom.

'What do you want?'

He looked sheepish as he always did, he muttered something, 'Warn you . . .'

Her lighter clicked as she lit herself a cigarette, 'Warn me about what?'

He seemed more tongue-tied than ever.

'Spit it out, for God's sake. I've got someone coming round.'

'Don't let anyone in tonight.' He had worked himself up into a state.

'Whatever do you mean?'

'It's not safe, Pam. I'm . . . concerned about you.'

She laughed at him. 'It's a little late for that.'

He got her by the arm then, 'Get off me. What d'you want?'

'You'd best come with me.'

'To Starveall. You're joking!'

He tried to pull her to the door but she resisted him.

'At this hour. What's this all about? It's not Morality, is it?'

The seriousness of whatever it was began to dawn. She took the housecoat off, he turned away. 'It's all right. I'll come in a minute. Don't run off.'

The back door opened again.

'Effin B!'

Frankie Pierce walked straight into the cottage.

'Hang on. Let me cover myself.'

But Frankie ignored her. 'Scarper,' he told Tom, 'get off,' and legged it up the stairs.

'Get dressed,' Frankie told Pam. 'I'm taking you down mum's.'

'You're what!'

He grabbed her, but she tried to wriggle away from him.

'Shut up,' he said, 'don't argue, don't speak. No one's going to touch you if you do just what we say.'

While she dressed he pulled the curtains, 'We'll leave the lights, you made it very cosy.' He took her out the back door, leaving it on the latch. For safety's sake, his working hand held tight across her mouth.

It turned out there were two of them. Ranelagh, who just perhaps had a whiff of something, had brought a mate up with him. Neither got as far as Carver. They were taken out, as Lydney neatly put it, as the road dips down beyond Hooley's, a half mile from Midway. From here the caddy van freewheeled – Lydney, Stephen and Ralph in front on the bench seat, the corpses of the soldiers slid in on top of fertiliser bags in the back – in moonlit silence, east-wards, still on Childe land, across a field of rough grazing to where the lip of the disused quarry mouth was fenced off by barbed wire. They rolled the bodies beneath the wire, then clambered down the loose stone workings. Without the need of torchlight, sho-vels, hidden earlier, were taken up and the three of them worked, with just the odd sound of steel scraping on stone, covering the two bodies with layers of sodden refuse from the dump.

Getting back up the quarry face proved more difficult. Tufts of grass came away in their hands, stones slithered where they tried for a foothold, nails broke, hearts pounded with fear and effort as they heaved themselves up to that blessed crust of top soil on the lip. They lay panting among the thistles and the cow pats before crawling on their bellies to the van.

Lydney made it first, then Ralph joined him. Stephen did not appear. The two men waited. In the moonlight, Ralph looked questioningly at Lydney but Lydney shrugged his shoulders, shook his head. They waited a further five minutes then continued as they had planned.

Lydney steered as Ralph pushed the van two hundred yards across the field, through the gate and back on to the track. Working quietly in the darkness, they jacked the van up and removed the tyre and then, taking it and the fertiliser bags out of the back, began the walk back up to Carver Hill. Only now did they start whispering, walking in single file along the mound of grass that grew in the middle of the rutted track. Stephen might have been in front of them, or close behind. Ralph carried the bags and the tyre, Lydney held the gun.

'He got up the face all right?' he asked Ralph.

'I thought he was with you.'

'No, he wasn't with me.'

Ralph struck a match with shaking fingers. He looked at Lydney in the light of it. Lydney shrugged.

'As cool as a cucumber,' Ralph said later to his brother Frankie as he crawled into his bed.

'He thought Stephen was with me. That's what he said. I thought Stephen was with him.'

'You lost him then?' Frankie commented.

'Looks bloody like it,' Ralph said.

Three

TWELVE

'People die of grief,' Morality told Dora, 'they just wither up. The sap goes clean out of them, like autumn leaves . . .' The chink of bottles sounded the reformation of the dressing table: 'The oomph goes out of them' Morality pushed down one of her cuticles with a matchstick, searching for the right word, 'it evaporates. It happens with animals, especially hens . . .'

Dora regretted the feelings she had about Stephen in the cottage. She would tell him straight out that she was sorry. She should have been more understanding but then she'd been so anxious for so long. There were things they had to talk about, sort out between them. But he had no reason to doubt her, every feeling she ever had for him remained intact.

She was sorry, she expected him at any moment, the warm, worn smoothness of the yard gate under her palm; from here she would catch first sight of Stephen coming back.

Flaying to stand there and be watched.

'Any news?'

That old pain in her side, like a stitch but not a stitch.

'Terrible.' Netty making her a cup of tea she didn't

want, putting a biscuit on the saucer. A biscuit really helps. 'Terrible,' but she would just mention the blackcurrants, 'Downright wicked' to let them go to waste. Dora wouldn't want to be bothered with . . . 'Have a good cry.' Netty mentally ran a kitchen fork through the branches for the berries, that tart smell as you bruise the leaves. 'It's the not knowing . . . in normal times but now . . .' 'Alice always said, "You take them Netty, before anybody else does." She said to me, I don't how many times, "I tell you Netty, no one can touch you when it comes to making jam."'

'A lovers' tiff? Every married couple, she should know . . .' 'A good year for currants and after currants, plums,' 'And they were just starting off, weren't they? How many months? Six months, there's the pity of it, and Maggie expecting . . .'

Oh warmed by disaster, the chorus of Carver women. Gratified by her misfortune!

She didn't catch them talking about her because they didn't even have to use language to discuss it and Dora didn't need to overhear to know. Their silence was more eloquent than any underhum of talk; their opinions on the matter were plain to see. There, in the fold of their arms, in the slope of their sagging bosoms, in the ties of an overall. In the sweeping of their steps, in the picking off and discarding of the dead leaves of the geranium.

She searched in the mess of their adjoining bedrooms for a note. She sat on his chair beneath the angel ceiling, looked outwards for an explanation. She went to bed in a cardigan and socks. Desolation. It felt . . . it felt as if the background had all gone.

Sunshine, lots of it, well of course. The frames of the windows making diagonal lines across the shutters, dust in motes. When she walked about the upstairs of the house she heard the sound of her own feet tapping.

Flaying to be stared at.

Walked the upstairs of the house, saw Tom Allen hose the yard down. Dog barked. Silence.

Walked. Walked back into her husband's room, just the remains of an old fire in the grate. Bit along her thumbnail, looked at herself in his mirror, opened the hanging cupboard, looked at the clothes on the pegs and hangers but didn't touch the material.

Lydney unlocked the door of his office, relocked it. Maggie going out with a bucket to open up and feed the hens. Maggie walked – 'Dear love her,' Netty said – walked as if frightened of falling down.

And Dora would like to push her down and keep her down, head under the water.

Dora sat on Stephen's chair on the long gallery, put her hand down the side of it, looking for something, she wouldn't stop looking, to stop looking would be wrong.

The garden, a field, all long grass and dandelion puffs. Part of the white lilac had fallen into the purple and they lay there flowering horizontally together. Joke time in the clock's strike. The chair's upholstery warm from the sun through the window. She pulled a loose thread from the chair cover and twirled it like embroidery silk to make a knot, put the knot into her mouth and sucked it.

High heels tapping, Morality, her little shadow, lit a cigarette behind her, 'They're from the shop.'

She smoked contentedly. They were Stephen's.

'You can't stop here all day.' Morality bored easily, 'May I have one?' To touch something of his.

Morality was delighted, she lit it from hers, 'Are you going to do something, Dora? What are you going to do?'

Dora on the unmade bed. Tap, slide, tap. Beyond the window, silence.

'Lydney says they're going to leave the weather-boarding now.'

Morality pairing up discarded shoes.

'Shall I leave you a cigarette, Dora?'

'Just go.'

Dora falling into the hanging cupboard, pulling down his clothes. Joke time, blackbirds. Water flowed from the well into the pipes and filled the tanks. New day. When he came back she wouldn't ask him what had happened. She'd play it as her mother played it, iron the shirts, feed the belly, 'I didn't know when to expect you, I'm afraid this is a bit dried up.'

She went downstairs to get some coffee, but Cuffe had arrived. She heard his whining voice coming from the kitchen, couldn't face him, went back to her own room. Looked in the cupboard again, Stephen. Shoes off, down into the big bed.

Cold in the marrow, something deep inside her shrivelling up. Stop it, stop it, stop it. Important to stop it. Just stop it, Dora, don't let go.

Inside her, within her, in the centre of her was something like a fir cone before it opens up; when they'd made love he'd touched that. Tilting cone, beyond lust or satisfaction, he'd touched that. 'Something inside me died doctor,' the cone, the tilting cone, the cone that never fully opened, he'd touched that.

Night and the moon between the curtains. Dora made a list.

S. has left me.

S. has run away.

S. is dead.

'Caught up in something I shouldn't wonder.'

S. has been arrested.

S. is injured somewhere and I can't go to help him.

S. has gone because Maggie Frere is having his baby. Of all the lines this line was the hardest for her to write.

Action

Ask Lydney about it.

Go to town.

Do nothing that would arouse suspicion.

Sit tight.

Only when she was sure that Cuffe was in bed did she venture down the stairs. Out into the warm air, black night. He wasn't dead. She was sure that he was there somewhere. If she called in the night like an owl he'd hear her. Near her, she was sure. She had to say what he wanted her to say when they whitewashed the room together. That it didn't matter what he'd done or what he did. She had to make the lie, the lie that was required of her. She had to tell him that she trusted him, say the lie out loud into the night.

In the empty kitchen at the table with a bowl of pickings from the fridge in front of her, still untouched. A note for her to say that Father Cuffe was staying. Great.

Morality brought a cup of tea, set it down clumsily on the bedside table, a bit spilt.

'Maggie's sick again and so is Father Cuffe. I'll get the meals and that if you pay me for it.'

'Go away, Morality.'

'Pardon me for breathing.' Morality flounced out.

Don't do anything that might arouse suspicion, yet Dora had decided: she would go to town.

'I can let you have a can of petrol if it will help,' said Lydney. Solicitous. He had come up while she was in the garage. Generous. He was lending her the van. Lydney, there. There, just as he used to be when she went to open the shutters, that long-ago winter, his hand on the tongs when a log fell from the fire; now he gave her a can of petrol, 'just in case'.

'What do you mean?' she turned on him. 'Let me have! What do you mean?' She loathed him, 'just in case?'

'I think you know . . . restrictions and road blocks and . . .'

'Just let me have the can.' She leant against the dark blue van as he locked and unlocked the store shed. Tom Allen tried to catch her eye but she ignored him; she hated, hated, hated everyone's sympathy.

'I'm sorry you're upset.' Lydney, unscrewing the petrol cap.

'Oh Christ, just fill it up!'

'Best to take care.'

She didn't care what happened to her.

Morality looked exactly as if she'd been asked to

dress up as a prostitute; a tight black skirt, the back
vent of which had been repaired with lighter thread,
and a low cut, turquoise chenille top slipping off her
shoulders, showing the greasy black strap of her bra.
Talking as they drove through the countryside, a trail
of her cigarette ash from the carpet to the window.

Everyone was ill. Not Netty or Enda, well they
were never ill. Not the twins or Ralph and Frankie
or Mrs P come to that, or Tom. But Maggie was
and Morality's mum was and so was Father Cuffe.
Cuffe was suffering from what Netty called a summer
'flu, Maggie was as sick as a dog again and Pam was
having a nervous breakdown.

'Morality!'

'It's true! She wants to lie down all the time and
she can't stop crying. She won't talk to me any more,
she won't speak.'

Dora took the news in silence.

'Don't say you're sorry nor nothing. You never
think of anyone but yourself.'

'I am sorry.'

'Smoothie chops has done a bunk. That soldier.
That's the bottom and the top.' Morality drew hard
on her cigarette. 'She'll probably get over it.' Morality ever practical who thought she'd seen it all before,
'Just take a bit of time, I suppose.'

'I am sorry, Morality.'

'I know.'

After this Morality grew quiet and they drove
along the twisting road in silence. Dora hadn't really
looked at Morality for days. Now she did she saw
with guilt that beneath the painted-in eyebrows the
eyes were ringed and red.

'Cuffe moved in almost a week ago.' Morality had caught Dora's glance and begun to talk again to cover her embarrassment. 'He moved in the same day as . . .'

'It's all right. Say it.'

'He thinks he got a bug from all the driving round he's made to do and Maggie's been complaining like mad about it because, with you not coming down or anything, it's her mum's had to do the extra work. Cuffe says his legs have gone weak, he has to have everything brought to him. His legs will hardly support him, so he says. Maggie can't keep anything down, Mrs Pierce says it means . . . carrying it in front, a boy. Could be twins but then that often skips a generation.'

Tough on Dora was what they all said secretly. Only imagine! A double blow if it were twins.

Dora expected to be stopped as she had been with Lydney but the road was clear all the way. After an hour's drive they began to see water through the gaps in the trees. The road was like a switchback around the lakes. Dora tried and kept drawing back from overtaking. They got behind a farmer driving an old and rusted pick-up, its tailboard tied with baling twine and wire.

'Why don't you overtake it?' Morality suggested as Dora began to snort and swear.

'Because I can't.'

'I can't drive.'

'Shut up then.'

The journey got slower and slower and she nearly drove into the back of the pick-up as a soldier waved them down, making a turning motion with his hand.

They could see the soldier having a word with the farmer. Dora yanked on the hand brake, grabbed her papers and got out, slamming the van door. Morality, arranging her skirt, followed. There were cat-calls from behind the hedge.

'Is this a block or what?'

The soldier looked at her papers, at Morality and at the number of the van.

'You won't get in this way,' he said, quite nicely.

'Why?'

'The bridge is gone. It's been gone a week.'

He pointed and yes, Dora could see for herself, no bridge.

'I have to go to town.'

'Well, you'll have to go the other way then.'

Morality offered Dora her lit cigarette, her answer to every crisis. Dora waved it away.

'How? How do I go the other way?' she asked pathetically.

'All the way round and come back in.'

'If you want to add twenty-five mile to your journey,' said the farmer, very smug.

Dora ignored him, asked the soldier, 'That bridge is okay?'

'I told you.'

Dora leant against the van, sagging. The pick-up turned tediously in the road.

'I'll follow you,' she said to the farmer who was leering at Morality, almost dribbling.

'Twenty-five mile round! I shan't be going.' Dora winced with frustration. 'You got a tankful you go ahead.'

'I haven't got a tankful.'

The farmer let the pick-up into gear again.

'Hang on. Just a minute. Please,' she said. The farmer looked through Dora at Morality, 'You're giving up then?'

'Reckon I got no choice.'

'Oh, go on then!' Dora gave the man a filthy look, stood there, hopeless by the van. Now Morality looked expectantly at her like a dog. 'Okay. Back in the van. Wasted journey.'

'You're never giving up!'

Dora hardly gave Morality time to get in, drove off fast, 'Yes. I'm giving up.'

'You've got that can of petrol.'

'Shut up.'

'But I saw Lydney . . .'

Dora braked hard in top gear, skidding halfway out across the road. She grabbed Morality by the arm, speaking very slowly, 'I have decided not to go because I don't know what I'm going for. Because it would take an age to get there. Because I can't run back to Mill Street and ask for help. Because . . .'

'All right, all right, you're hurting me!'

'Christ!' Dora got back on to the right side of the road, squealing around the corners, driving until the lakes were out of sight.

'You could overtake anything if you can drive this fast.'

'Shut up!'

They passed a group of stragglers on the road, a mother with several children, one of the children cradling a baby,

'Don't look at them,' Dora instructed Morality. 'I'm not stopping. Don't even look!'

Ten miles more and she did stop, pulling into the side of the road, laying her hot face on the steering wheel, 'I'll have that cigarette now.'

Morality was pleased with her again.

'I'm sorry,' Dora said.

'It's all right.'

'The soldier said the bridge had been gone at least a week,' Dora said as they drove on again. 'One can of petrol Lydney gave me. One can. Lydney must have known about the bridge.'

'D'you think so?'

'Don't say anything,' she warned Morality on the home stretch, turning up from Midway. She pinched her arm again to get the message through to her, 'Don't say anything at all.'

She locked the van and put the keys in her pocket; she locked the petrol cap. Her eye caught something in the corner of the barn half hidden by a torn tarpaulin. Cuffe's Lambretta. She wasn't having that!

Cuffe had made his quarters downstairs at the back of the house. A bed had been put in a little anteroom for him to use when he needed it, but he had spread himself to the adjoining parlour, where Alice's piano gathered dust.

He couldn't talk to anyone, he couldn't talk to the PKFs, he couldn't talk to Lydney, he couldn't talk to God. Terror had made his legs weak so that he couldn't run away. Terror had scattered the few wits he once had about him.

He had to go to Lydney for the keys to the churches at Carver, Midway, New Mills. He had fallen as low as it was possible to fall, and for the last week he had

135

lain prostrated on this bed. Lydney and his likes had him where they wanted him, used the churches for their own devices. Even his salary from the PKFs had been intercepted, he had to beg Lydney for a share of it, enough to die on, he thought miserably. He cleaved to Dora, but now it seemed she too had deserted him until this afternoon. He felt a flicker of hope as he recognised her approaching step.

The room was bachelor sweaty, the curtain half-drawn out of idleness or a desire for darkness, Cuffe's helmet and gloves next to a vase in which the flowers were smelly and dead. It was fetid – the remains of a tray of food, crusts of bread balanced on the saucer, a line of old tea visible in a cup. Dora picked the flowers out of the vase, 'These stink!' she hurled them at the wastepaper basket, foul water dripped across the carpet. Cuffe's wide face gleamed in the half-darkness. He was unshaven and lay on the sofa in at least the top half of his clothes. He sat up quickly enough when she came in, dog eyes looking up at her, 'Please. Please. Don't worry on my behalf. I've everything I need. Thank you. Thank you very much. I don't want to be any trouble.'

She advanced on him, bore down upon the grisly little man.

'This summer weather,' he pleaded with her, 'Blowing hot and cold,' and quite suddenly he burst into tears.

Dora banged and clattered to cover her embarrassment, collecting the cups and saucers and the plates with plenty of 'Honestlys', 'Reallys', and 'For God's sakes!'

'Why don't you get properly into bed if you're ill?' she asked unkindly.

'I . . .'

She didn't give him time to answer. She marched into the other room. It was easy to see why. The bed in the next room was crumpled-up and horrible. Netty, who complained of doing everything, had obviously done fuck-all. Out of common courtesy to another human being, Dora fetched fresh sheets, then began to strip the bed, all the while from the adjoining room came the pathetic squeak of the priest protesting. The mattress was a thin, lumpy thing, Dora groaned her zoo groan, every domestic task leading to another.

'Christ, I think we can do better than this.'

She kicked the old sheets into the corridor, struggled with the pillow cases, greasy with some kind of hair oil, picked up the mound of bedding and carried the lot down the passageway, turning her nose up at the smell.

Netty, Maggie and Mrs Pierce were cackling in her kitchen. They looked surprised to see her, stopped talking as usual the moment she came in. She dumped the sheets on the table between them, 'I'd like some help carrying down a mattress from upstairs. Someone,' she looked at Maggie with loathing, 'someone with plenty of strength in their arms and legs.'

Maggie looked at her mother but it was old Mrs Pierce of the wavy-edged red cardigan who pulled herself up from the table, wiping her hands on her drooping skirt. They were eating what looked like the bones of a chicken.

'Late lunch or early tea?'

'Taking it easy too soon,' said Mrs Pierce before they were out of earshot of the kitchen. 'I told her, and I told Netty. She'll be a great fat lump and then have trouble later on. Bloody men, they make you pay for it,' she continued, surprisingly sprightly, up the stairs. 'You're young, you'll see. This for the priest is it? Don't think it's right myself, bothering with him. I haven't been upstairs in this house for I don't know how long. Gone to rack something terrible,' she said as they entered the back bedrooms that looked on to the yard. 'Not going to be set right not in our lifetime, not with your husband gone. We going to give him this good cover to muck up? Put this good cover in the press and give him some old thing.' She took the corners of the cover Dora had taken down and refolded it efficiently, the backs of her hands freckled, the scrawny arms.

'I know what's in here.' She rummaged in the cupboard. 'Probably put it in here myself more than twenty years ago. It's a long time since I been up here mind. Alice had her problems, there's no denying that, and your husband said how he didn't like anyone in the upstairs of the house. He says we all live together downstairs but upstairs is for privacy . . . what he wants privacy for I don't know but we're not all made alike.'

On she went, quite amiably: Stephen's father, Stephen's grandfather, the young wife who'd died of seven-day disease.

'Happened to all sorts and the graveyard's a witness to it, those that raised their children were the lucky ones.'

As they turned the corner of the stairs, carrying the

mattress and the quilt down between them, 'Time's a healer,' she said, the first kind words Dora had yet heard.

She was vicious to the priest however, quite obviously did not approve, 'You all right then?' she asked curtly.

Cuffe coughed just once to prove he wasn't. Mrs Pierce considered him with disdain and took up the conversation where she had left off, 'So after she died he had everyone in sight.' Dora had lost the thread but it didn't matter. 'No one was safe from that one. He fancied me, course I was widowed young. Hark at her you say but we all look better with a full set of teeth. Your Stephen got his grandfather's side, if you don't mind me saying so. Now his father . . . You came upstairs in the old man's time and you got more'n a flick round with a duster.

'No one ever made this much mess,' she said for the priest's benefit. 'Mind on higher things?'

'These downstairs rooms aren't healthy. This house got no proper foundations, that's the bottom and the top. All right at the front but not the back going into this wet bank.' She punched the pillows with her fist. 'The Sevens and The Bottoms were built some time later on . . .

'Don't see me in church,' she said to Cuffe, handing him a blanket. He wrapped it around himself and hopped ignominiously into the adjoining room.

'He got no night things,' she whispered to Dora.

'You got no night things, Father?'

Cuffe pulled the clean sheets right up to his neck.

'We'll leave you to it then. See if you gets better in here shall we? You want the window left open?

139

You want the curtains drawn together or pulled back?
There you are, handsome is as handsome does.

'You couldn't get through to your father's then?'
she said leaving Cuffe's door lightly on the latch.
'You tried your best even if it were a waste of petrol.
I'd be just the same if anything happened, family's
family when all's said.'

THIRTEEN

People die of grief on a regular basis, but the late
flowering of Nat Lydney was something to behold.
He had moved himself, morning by morning, bit by
bit, afternoon by late afternoon, into the best and the
largest downstairs room of the house. The room with
Aunt Sadie's grandfather clock in it, the room that
led out to the monkey puzzle in the garden, the room
where the violet silk curtains, Alice's passion, hung
in fraying shreds.

He moved himself in for Dora's sake: he was her
protector.

The yard office she had watched him unlock so
many times now remained locked. The centre of
operations had changed. Lydney had moved in: for
her safety. She needed a man in the house.

It was time and motion, it was management, it was
sensible and efficient: the honourable step.

Now that he was, once more, in charge of things
he positioned himself at Stephen's desk. He sat where
Stephen had sat. He was available should she require
his services: tongs, shutters, shoulder to cry on . . .

And Dora had no energy to prevent it. At the sight
of the desk, the paperclips, the bowl of sharpened
pencils, she felt weak. If it wasn't rather terrifying it

would have been amusing because, in some way, Lydney was made more vulnerable by this latest, most ambitious, leap.

Sitting at the desk, locking up at night – he enjoyed it all so much. The sharpened pencils, like little spears, honestly amazed her. So difficult to take him seriously, knowing that the aftershave was in the bottom drawer . . .

With Stephen off the premises, Lydney now specialised in secret glances full of tender meaning, squeezing her hand like a mason with a message, 'With my help you'll pull through.'

Flirtatious behaviour is a thing of the past. Let's not mention it again. Dora is on a pedestal now, martyr-saint: approaches to her are circumspect, thoroughly gallant. Should she ask for calves' foot jelly or beef tea, or to be wrapped from head to toe in scented linen bandages, it would not be too much.

And Dora knew absolutely nothing about farming, about fat lambs, would prefer not to come face to face with a cow. Work, so nearly completed, had stopped at The Sevens. What was she expected to do about it, scale the ladder with a hammer clamped between her teeth? Nails rusted where they had fallen, grass grew up and covered the fallen brace. Lydney had Stephen's desk, the chorus had commandeered the kitchen.

'Woe to Julietta who married in haste to a man from a different tribe! Woe! Woe! Woe!'

Back to the beginning.

She had slept and slept at the beginning, now she couldn't sleep. She rambled about upstairs, little ritu-

als of watching and the sound of just her own feet –
tap, tap, tap. Often she would lie on the bed with
her clothes on during the daytime, the list she'd made
beside her on the bedside table. She longed to talk to
Stephen about a host of inconsequential things, silly
small things, details.

'I've taken the quilt off the bed now. The camellias
are absolutely hopeless, bud but won't come out. I
am keeping going, laid out but not prostrated.'

The longing just to speak to him grew as each day
slowly, slowly, passed. She began to write him little
notes.

'Wednesday.'

Sometimes she got no further than the day of the
week, but she kept each one, hiding them between
the pages of a book.

Something had gone wrong with the big trailer,
she could see it jacked up in the middle of the yard.
Tom Allen wheeled his barrow around it – squeak,
squeak, squeak, squeak.

He looked very cowed and miserable these days,
not much to choose between him and the grisly
priest. All his tasks seemed interminable, he moved
about the yard like a man who has been reduced. He
had never liked Nat Lydney; he once told Dora that
if Lydney came into the kitchen at meal time the food
stuck in his throat. Dora had always thought of Tom
as dumb but sensitive, to be handled in the way that
he had handled the kittens, but she hadn't got time
for dumbness or for sensitivity any more. She muttered at the window as she watched him, 'Stupid,
lugubrious old sheep!'

Lydney loved to castigate and boss him, could

always come up with something long-winded and nasty, something that would hack his hands and crick his back, something grim for him to do. Today's curse was to build a bonfire, Tom bringing piles of stuff out from the cobwebbed corners of old outhouses, pushing the barrow – squeak, squeak, squeak.

'For Christ's sake oil that barrow!' Dora bearing down, yelling at him as she crossed the yard.

'And you can't have that, or that, or those!' She rescued, fell upon, Stephen's single wellingtons, old overalls, ripped coats.

'Lydney!' she squawked, pummelling Tom in a sudden rage with a squashed straw hat.

'Who said you could burn all this? I don't want anything burnt that I haven't authorised.' She felt ridiculous even as she spoke the word.

'Do you hear me? All of you!' Tears poured down her cheeks. At long last she was crying. She hugged the wellington and the oily overall, the squashed straw hat.

'How dare you, how dare you! I hate you all! He's only missing . . .' she said as Mrs Pierce wearing a hat that ought to have been incinerated, gathered her up and took her through the apple-smelling scullery.

'Missing,' she turned in the old woman's arms and yelled back at the lot of them, 'Missing. Not dead!'

It was a big, foul-smelling bonfire – rubber tyres and other rubbish, the priest's old mattress – stoked and poked at by the stupid sheep. Morality would have nothing to do with anything that might get her hands dirty and had gone off. Dora brought a kitchen chair out and sat and watched the sparks rising and dying in the black-purple summer sky.

Lydney gave her the key to the church because she asked for it, but he went up there first to make sure nothing was amiss.

'Please God, make Stephen come back to me and make Maggie's baby a mistake.' Dora believed in God again, she knelt right up to pray. 'Or, even if it isn't a mistake, it doesn't matter as long as he comes back.'

Outside the church summer heat came full blast on her head and shoulders, past the chaotic yews which had slung themselves over and broken the churchyard wall. She went straight to Stephen's room as if, after all this time, she might find some evidence against him. He hadn't slept with her in here, had he? Hadn't talked about Dora to her, in here? She looked across at the window. Go on Dora, jump!

If Stephen was dead and Maggie's baby was his, then there would be something of Stephen left, and she could . . . could what? Bring herself to love the baby? She flung his cupboard door open, she kicked out at the clothes and then she touched them and she smelt them and she held them in her arms. She dreamt she burnt his cupboard and his clothes.

She woke up to the smell of burning, to disturbing, foreign noises downstairs. She counted six PKFs, but there were others posted at the doors. There was so much noise in the big room that they didn't hear her instinctive protest as she reached the corner of the stairs. Two pushed past her without explanation and when she reached the foot of the stairs another one grabbed her, shoved her into the sitting room and on to a chair. When she went on asking and protesting, he put the nozzle of his rifle between her breasts.

'Shut up.'

Maggie, Morality, all the Pierces, Pam, Netty and Enda and the twins, Father Cuffe – all were assembled in the chaos of the room, only Nat Lydney was missing.

Papers everywhere like a burglary, drawers and ink, the shards of Stephen's fountain pen snapped under someone's boot. Neat files picked up, splayed out, drawings, the back torn off the atlas, wood ash spilling on to the floor. Dora watched amazed as one middle-aged, very ordinary soldier – you would only be frightened of him because he had a gun – pulled the old violet curtains off the wall; lathe and plaster crumbling, flaking to the floor.

They sat in a line like spectators. The demented twin looked excited, almost bounced in his chair. She asked where Lydney was and from the far end of the line of chairs, Mrs Pierce, red cardigan over her nightdress, slippers, made a gone away look with her eyes before the soldier slapped Dora hard across the cheek, his wedding ring catching the corner of her mouth. Blood. A drawer was thrown over the banisters, mothballs rolled, the curtain soldier peed over Lydney's papers, on and on, steaming like a horse. The sound of heavy boots and splintering wood and laughter and swearing and Mrs Pierce, sobbing as she wet herself, a little pool gathering around her slippered feet.

The taste of blood, the smell of urine mixed with fire. Dora's tooth jumped where the soldier had struck her, her legs shook and her hands fluttered in her lap. Father Cuffe set up a moan – typical of him – and Dora sensed Maggie who was next to him, his noise exposing her, Maggie's fear. Dora concentrated all her force on Maggie then, exposed by the noise and fuss the priest was making, his crying drawing attention to that area of the room. Dora dared to move her head for Maggie's sake, saw Maggie's eyes, wild like cow's eyes and Dora moved her eyes begging Maggie to lower hers, moving her eyes in an effort to communicate that somehow it would be better, safer, not to meet the soldiers' eyes, look down.

Joke time, normality and anarchy entwined. The soldiers brought things from the back and threw things down the stairs. Armfuls were taken out and she thought, they are at least using the front door. The door wide open to the early morning, birdsong and the flowers still standing in the vase in all this extraordinary and frightening, already growing familiar, sound of banging and crashing, breaking up.

A long time and a short time: thoughts snagged, eyes trained on detail, the wobble of the water in the glass vase as a soldier jostled the table. The new sound of things smashing through the windows of the angel gallery, shattering and thudding as they hit the grass and stones below. The line of them all, eyes lowered; not to look, only to listen, provided some kind of a shell, though the gun at Dora's breast made her sit upright and she could smell the man who held it there. Dora looking down, for so long, for so short a time, at his legs. She could remake those dark blue trousers in that same material. She could see the line of the inside seam and the tear, there, just beginning at the pocket and the belt on the last hole. He was thin, she thought, thinner than when he was issued with those trousers.

Aunt Sadie's clock was so enormous that one almost didn't notice it; they had overlooked it, now they saw it and, in one gesture, pushed it off the wall. It fell like a tree on its face across the floor, shattered glass in the sunlight from the open door.

'Where are they, bitch of all bitches?' he was talking to Dora, asking her a question.

'I'll hit you.'

But another stopped him. The gun was now under her chin, her head turned up to the ceiling. She heard all the taps running at once, she thought of her list on the bedside table, her notes to Stephen upstairs in a book.

'Where's your husband?'

'I truly don't . . .'

He hit her anyway: 'Playing dumb are we?'

Honestly, what a word.

'Cow.' He moved his gun away from her chin, he shoved it up beneath her nightdress, the barrel scratched along the inside of her leg. She thought of herself in the third person, 'If he pokes that inside her, she is going to faint.'

Her head was free and she moved it and looked along the row of people and tried to tell them that this wouldn't go on very long. They did this to the Bonbon, he survived. Too dumb to . . . playing . . . her hands were off again, with enormous effort she picked up the thread. That soon the soldiers would be called away. That something else would happen to stop this going on. She was sitting on the back of her nightdress, he couldn't lift it up that far.

'Scrawny, isn't she?' said one.

Lydney is going to walk through the front door or come in from the back at any moment now. Tom Allen will arrive, this will stop.

She had to talk, that's what one did on these occasions, but not the sort of talk that might inflame the situation, not the sort of talk that might annoy. Somehow judge the mood, the atmosphere, get it right Dora because you can't afford to get it wrong. But how could you talk if it meant you had to stop thinking? When thinking made you feel so . . . well, so peculiarly relaxed. Her hands were calm now, nothing hurt, it had gone on for a long time and what she was thinking was remarkably interesting once you got into it, a sort of reverie, dangerous she knew, dangerous but too delicious to forgo. Down, down, down, down, into the cool deep water: is it over like this, is this what happens . . . they were hardly even questions. A question has an edge to it, all she felt was gentle, gentle slope. So this is it, a sort of swooning curiosity, almost beyond, outside oneself. Down, down and into the deep cool water: I've wondered about my life and death and is it this, do I recognise any part of what is happening, is there anything at all familiar about the landscape I'm now in?

'Cat got your bitching tongue?' said trousers and then Mrs Pierce groaned as she fell or was pushed from her chair to smash, like the clock on the floor and Dora got it.

'Woopsiedaisy!' breaking the surface of the water, coming up, roaring back into the light.

'Don't come here looking for salt!' she bellowed at them. 'Salt! Salt! Salt! Salt!' She stretched out her hands and grabbed the blue serge trousers, trying to stand up. Turning awkwardly in her chair, raising herself up.

'My brother's gone away. Don't hurt me,' she said putting her hand to the barrel of the gun and pushing it away from her, 'My brother's gone away.'

'Your husband . . .'

She held on to his trouser leg. 'My brother's gone away. Gone away.' In a sing-song voice that was actually gaining confidence. 'All gone.'

She put her head forward, 'Woopsiedaisy!' until her head was on his legs.

'You coming home with me? You coming home?' she called across Alice's sitting room, 'You coming home with me?'

'Bloody hell,' the soldier said.

'You tell me what you want? My brother's gone away.'

The PKFs gathered in the room now. Trousers ran his fingers through his fringe. She'd always remember that fringe, those trousers.

It was almost over now, wasn't it, beginning to be over now. The end of noise, time to survey the mess and see if you've forgotten anything, anything intact, anything left to crush or break or smash. One of them put a clock weight in his pocket, another aimed a kick at one of Dora's cats, but the viciousness had gone out of the morning, out of the kick, only the sound of birdsong and the running taps.

'Dora wants a cosy time!' she screamed after them. 'Who's going to cosy Dora down?'

'Bitches,' one said. Just a comment, no conviction.

Dora wandered after trousers, the palm of her hand beneath one breast, the other rubbing the thin cloth of her nightdress rhythmically against her groin, 'Don't leave me. Don't go. Don't leave Dora.'

She knew it was almost over, she put everything into it, she raised the cry she'd wanted to make when Stephen left.

'Don't leave me! Don't! Don't! Don't! Don't go!'

Four

FOURTEEN

Dora looks okay. The 'Oh, so you're back then?', and the 'What did I tell you?' and the 'Don't say we didn't warn you' phase is over. Dora can just about stop herself from skewering her father to his chair as he peels his fruit, garrotting her mother as she bends into the oven. Dora sleeps late in the morning at Mill Street, then walks uptown to the cleaners after lunch, where, beyond the racks of clothes, she is pressing other people's pleats. The smells of chemical fluids, the sounds of conversations across the counter. Dora is behind the scenes, damping first then ironing, a quiet worker bee who switches without argument when special orders, uniforms, upset the rhythm of the shop.

At ten to six she changes one overall for another, drinks coffee in a steamed-up café in The Hollow and then out into the cold again to the cinema, where she works as an usherette. She likes the darkness, it's darkness that she really loves. Between shows she sweeps between the rows of seats.

'Filthy bastards!' says another usherette, spitting on the floor, 'PFKs!'

'It doesn't bother me,' Dora says.

She smokes outside on the steps of the cinema, the

orange of the streetlights knocking out the hills. On Sunday afternoons she walks right down through the empty town to the hospital to visit the Bonbon with her friend, Morality Jukes. Contrary to expectations – those hulks shrunken by long-time hospital care – the Bonbon looks bigger than ever in his ground-floor ward. He is delighted to be there though the children's ward might be more appropriate for him. Only his hands look odd and soft, so very, very clean.

Dora and Morality smoke and chuck their cigarettes into the ornamental garden of winter shrubs at the main door of the hospital; one before they go in, another on their way out. Morality hates the smell of the hospital, Dora rather likes it. She pretends she's about to slip into an empty bed, or to run after the doctors and the nurses. It is and it isn't a joke. Something inside her is now dead. Her father sometimes tries to put his arm around her shoulders, but she always slips away. His touch, however fatherly and natural, affectionate, forgiving, is the same to her as that of the projectionist who walks her home after the last performance and once tried to kiss her in the doorway of the chemist's shop.

Morality isn't so particular, she likes town, likes working, likes men. She lied about her age to get her job and kept on lying, and in many ways seems older than the giggling girls she works with at the hair salon. She has many admirers but doesn't go overboard about any of them. Her mother has taken Maggie's job at The Rinkha and has a bedsit over the garage at Midway. Her letters, with their news of carpets and bed valances, an oval table and chairs that slotted perfectly into the bay window, are their only contact with the old world of Carver Hill. Pam writes in sticky biro, sends a postal order every week for her daughter's bottom drawer. Morality never lets a week go by without replying – what she says about her boyfriends is strictly edited but she is generous in her news of all her clients at the shop and ends admonishing her mother to, 'Take Care'.

September brings news that Mrs Pierce 'quietly passed away last Tuesday'; that Ralph and Frankie laid her out quite beautifully themselves, 'a crime to put her into the ground, the lovely things that she had on her.' Netty, rather touchingly, made her a wreath using bunches of Mrs Pierce's favourite pinks.

'Because they didn't cost nothing,' says Morality, who's got Netty's number good and proper.

Dora and Morality convey the news to the Bonbon, but he won't talk about the past. He will not talk about his life at Gobbins, is happy as he is in his ground-floor ward, looking out at the blank expanses of the lake.

Dora is earning money and not spending any, she only pays her parents for her keep. They are worried about her property and in October, to keep the peace, she visits their solicitor. There is a copy of the Allegiance Act in the waiting-room. The receptionist is off for lunch; Dora looks at the girl's feet, thinking how odd it is that people in town don't get dirty shoes.

The solicitor is about forty and is touched by the sight of Dora's overall beneath her coat.

'Your husband . . .' he draws his lips in sympathetically, she lights a cigarette. He gets an ashtray from his desk drawer. 'In five years' time you are free to remarry. Your property of course . . . application for compensation from the occupying force to be submitted within . . .'

At the cleaners there is a picture taped on to the back of the big machine – mountains and snow, a wooden chalet with a water wheel, a blue and birdless sky. She often looks at it. Now she looks at the solicitor's university degree framed on one side of the window, his second name.

He is talking about Carver. Like her father he is affectionate.

'I could drive you over there. I could drive you up there if it would be of any help?'

He waits for her to answer.

'Out of office hours. I'd be happy to.'

It isn't as easy as that.

Contrary to expectations the peace is holding well. Though congregation remains banned, petrol is no longer restricted and the curfew has been lifted. The hotel continues as the PFK headquarters, outside contractors work on a new barracks when the weather permits. Bests has reopened in a small way next to Casca's Five and Dime. The anniversary of Dora's wedding passes; Christmas trees are stacked outside the florist's. The florist is a girl she went to school with, this fazes Dora slightly as the girl beckons her in. Dora is thinking vaguely of Mrs Pierce. They say hello to each other. Dora doesn't really know what they say. After this greeting the conversation runs out of steam and Dora does nothing to fill the gaps, to help.

'Is there anything . . . ?'

'Pinks?'

'Carnations.'

The girl points them out, Dora picks a bunch of them, water dripping to the floor. She buries her nose deep in the still blossom, they don't smell. In town they sell flowers that don't smell.

'No thanks.'

She is spending hours in the shop and can't think of a way out of it although she must get to the cleaners before two.

'What sort of occasion?'

'For a grave,' says Dora.

'What about a Christmas wreath?'

'Too deadly,' Dora says.

She is smoking outside the cinema, seven o'clock on a weekday evening in the new year. Trade is very slack. Someone has followed her outside, Nat Lydney. She won't speak to him but he turns up after the show and insists on driving her home. The caddy van smells of aftershave. They drive in silence; he now insists on coming in. He wants to have a chat with her.

'After all this time?'

He looks her in the eye but she avoids his eye, making much of taking off and hanging up her coat.

'Morality wants to come back,' he says, 'I've had a word.'

Dora feels desperate, the rock surrounded by the water.

'It's up to her,' she says.

She won't look at Lydney, she thinks she's going to faint. She puts milk to boil in a saucepan.

'It's late.'

'Your parents have offered me the sitting room.'

Christ. He comes and stands beside her at the stove, like he opened the shutters for her, as he always was with her, close by, until she needed him of course.

'I hope we can be friends?' he says.

Fat chance. It's awful to have him in the kitchen. Dora wants to find somewhere to hide, her mind's gone absolutely blank. Again she says, 'It's late,' but she makes coffee for them both and they sit down opposite each other at her parents' tiny kitchen table.

'I came to see if you wanted anything?'

'No,' comes out like a mouse's squeak.

The sound of the spoon in his mug. You always hear the sound of the spoon. He puts it neatly to one side.

'I wondered if you wanted to come back?'

'To what?'

'I don't know why you left?'

'I left . . .' It's as if she has to think about it. Why bother to explain: that she'd left because the house was wrecked, because Stephen had gone, because Lydney had made them a target and he didn't even care. He just went off and left them to take the consequences.

'Why don't you just get out?' she says.

She stood up to make the message plain, but he didn't move.

'Have you seen the place? Have you seen it?'

'I'm living in it.'

Of course. Dora bundled a drying-cloth in her

hand then unbundled it, folded it, patted it to make it flat.

'The last thing I'd do is come back.'

'And they need you here?'

She will not speak to him.

'Well, perhaps they do need you?'

What Dora mustn't do is show emotion. She sat down again and put her hands around her coffee mug.

'Well. Come back, Dora.'

'Don't be stupid.'

'I'll leave you alone.' He put his hand across the table to touch her hand. She began to cry.

'When are you going to face up?' he asked, leaning very close.

He looked about the room, at Dora's uniform, 'Honestly Dora. What a show!'

She left the kitchen in an agony. She heard him downstairs, heard him turn off the kitchen light and go into the sitting room.

Down she went again, you never get a second chance, 'So you're running things up there?'

'Always did.'

She kicked a cupboard closed, which immediately came open again. He moved across the room close to her and shut it with a click.

'I'm running sheep at Bonbon's place. I've looked after the planting. In the spring I'm going to have a go at the house. We could do it together?'

'I'd rather die.'

'Just as you like.' His tone had changed. He seemed to accept her position, and yet she longed to go on talking, longed to. He made his bed ready.

'Be gone first thing,' he said, taking cushions off
the chairs.

FIFTEEN

The bus swings into the bends of the switchback road. Hold on to the strap! It lets its passengers off at Midway: the smell of the smoke from the cement works, from here, the field barn like a child's toy discarded on the skyline. The road zig-zags its way up the incline. After the turn to Starveall the road becomes a track, water runs down it making a deep rivulet, finding its own level on the way down. The mist hangs and you cannot see your nose before your face. How the track turns and turns, up, up. From here, on a clear day, you can see the two great lakes and the road snaking around them on the way to town. Walking up with hands in pockets and seeing your breath in front of your face, the cold like a black dog on your back.

A house that's lost its windows, like a mouth that's lost its teeth. Hardly recognisable from the front at all, the whole shape of the face altered, a death mask of a house. Beyond it, the burnt out and truncated church.

Oily puddles poach the gateway, the gatepost mended, bricks like new skin after a burn. Her hand on the cold gate remembers the warm smoothness of the gate in summer; silence, blasted by the rooks in the devastated churchyard, cawing what he'd called the shut of the day. She pulled her coat around her, sweeping past the pegs in the second scullery. She reckoned it would hurt him if she refused to take off her coat.

'I can find my own way.'

Lydney showed her into her old bedroom. He or someone had made up the bed.

'Just the one night then?' The hotelier.

'Yes.'

Looking at her, the bird's head on one side.

'You're looking well, Dora.' Wanting to get her name into the conversation, to say it, 'Dora'.

'I'll get some supper. I'll be around if you want a hand with anything.'

'I won't be wanting anything.'

He lingered in the doorway, he couldn't take his eyes off her.

'I expect you've heard already? Maggie's had her baby, a little girl.'

She didn't move at all at first in case he came back in. Stood there with her coat tight round her, waited till she heard his footfall on the stairs.

What looked like tidiness was crisis management. There were things in here that belonged to other rooms, odd chairs stacked against the walls. She wandered between the two adjoining rooms, looked into the garden once, then looked away again, forced herself to look into Stephen's cupboard, forced herself to touch the hanging clothes. She felt nothing. The list had gone of course, the notes she had written to Stephen, the book she'd hidden them in. She made some attempt to pack, then abandoned the idea. She would tell Lydney to set a match to it, that too might hurt. She lay on the bed, the cold up here, the silence – 'too cold for snow' – she felt that if she closed her eyes then she could sleep forever. Peace.

Lydney could do everything, she might have known he could also cook. What he couldn't do was to stop himself from showing off. A pheasant and a couple of woodcock, which made her turn her mouth down at the corners, far too much. Also she didn't like the way he carved so well or the way he spoke.

'How do you find it?'

The obvious reply was on her plate.

'Extravagant for two.' She saw she'd hurt him – great. Perhaps she should stick around, just so that she could wound him, regularly, once or twice a day? But how quiet it was, he didn't talk, the space all round them of empty rooms. He handed her the vegetables, his hands smelt of soap.

I can't do this. I thought I could, but I can't. It's too much for me, I'm in turmoil, I don't know what I'm doing. Lydney's face. I can't stand this, I want . . .

'Excuse me a moment.'

She walked into the corridor and down to the kitchen. Never had she seen the kitchen so shipshape. She ran the cold tap, the house so silent, she ran the tap, laid her forehead against the white stone of the sink. In a minute Lydney would come in behind her. She wiped her hands, wet her face all over and drew herself a glass of the cloudy, chalky water. She coughed as she walked up the corridor.

'Sorry,' she said, 'don't pat me on the back or

anything.' Christ don't touch me. 'Something went down the wrong way, that's all. I've ruined your lovely dinner. I'm sorry. A glass of water. I'll be all right in a minute.'

Whatever you do, she thought in desperation, don't touch me or look at me, particularly don't touch me because I'm going to collapse.

'Tell me about the farm?'

She dared not sleep. If she'd had the house to herself, if, if . . . If he hadn't been there she could have wandered about, but all she could do was open the window and look out. The last thing she wanted was to meet him in a corridor. She did not undress but sat in the darkness with the pillows at her back.

She heard him go out in the morning. Alone, she made a perfunctory check of the house. Rolls of rotting carpet where they'd run the taps, the ceiling down in Alice's sitting room. She saw, from the windows at the back, the patron saint and self-styled deliverer of Carver opening the door of the caddy van to take the twins down to the school!

How was she going to play this? How was she going to win this round?

She confronted him in his office, 'I won't sit down.'

Her hands in her pockets, freezing cold.

'Sit down, Dora.'

'No!' What was it about him that drove her raving mad like this? Everything. Everything about him drove her mad. She made an effort to compose herself; she wished Morality were up here with her, she could have done with a crisis cigarette.

'Look.' Breathe deeply. Standing by the door, quietly and sensibly, calmly, she opened her mouth

and out it all came in a rush, 'I want to end everything. Stop it. Shut the house up, set the farm, whatever. It's what I need to do.'

He looked unimpressed.

'I want an end to all of it. I've thought about it and
I've decided. For my sake, you must understand,
things have got to have an end.'

Silence.

'So, what I'm proposing is . . . what I'm saying
is, I think you'd better leave.'

'Sit down, Dora.'

I loathe you. 'I'd really rather stand.'

'I don't think you have thought this through,
Dora.'

'I have, believe me. I have.'

'You want to put four or five men out of a job?'

'No . . .'

'Well, that would be the consequence of such
action, wouldn't it? Four men out of a job. I'm building the place up, Dora. I told you last night. I'm
running sheep at Bonbon's, I'm over-wintering more
cattle this year than we've ever done. I've got plans.'

'Well, I'm sorry. These things happen.'

'People make them happen.'

'Okay.'

'Dora . . . think. Aren't you forgetting your
responsibilities?'

'Make me responsible? Why should I be responsible
for all this?'

'Because it's what Stephen would have wanted.'

The trump card. Dora pushed Stephen out of her
mind in order to go on.

'But see it from my position, Lydney. What's in it

for me? Oh it's great for you, that's obvious enough, but what's in it for me? I want an end to all of it.' Unruffled and most loathsome bird. 'I don't want to stay here.' Supercilious bastard sitting at his little desk. 'I'm not going to go along with this Lydney.' Was he smiling? 'I hate it here. I've always hated it.' Let him have it. 'I've always hated you.'

'We don't need to get on,' he said.

'Flaying to stand here and be watched.' Dora didn't give a damn who saw her, she stomped furiously around Carver Hill. No attempt had been made to reroof the church; in any case the idea of God in Carver was ridiculous. The building was full of leaves; she stepped in across burnt timbers, refusing to offer up a prayer, even a small one. The burning of the church had changed the landscape, the weatherboarding of the stumpy tower no longer stood out, pale, against the darkly rising hill.

Outside in the graveyard tiny cyclamen poked through the leaf mould beneath the yew trees; they did smell and there was something in their tinyness, pushing up through hard winter ground, that Dora decided she wasn't in the mood for. She stumped back down the short-cut to the house.

Netty was in the kitchen to catch the latest. Dora had been away a long time yet the top was still on the sugar canister, the kettle on the stove.

'I'll make a will,' thought Dora as she watched the old bat make the tea. 'For perpetuity. All soft fruit in my garden to Netty Frere.'

'Eight and a half pounds.'

It took a moment for Dora to surface from the world of jam.

'The baby. Congratulations. Yes I heard.'

'Just a passing visit?'

Oh yes just passing, one toured the western region and one passed Carver.

'That's it.'

Ralph and Frankie were lodging with Netty now, another little money spinner, 'Poor lambs couldn't boil an egg.'

Poor lambs.

'You've got your work cut out then?' had to be Dora's line.

'Devil makes work for idle hands,' was hers.

They drank their tea together, Dora's eyes wandered round the room. Everything was silence here, silence, and now that she had been away she could put a word to it, weight. The weight of a long past that tethered Carver people complacently to the view from their windows of sky and sheep and hill. The weight that gave them licence to judge, the weight which was their legacy, self-righteousness and self-congratulation they took in with their mother's milk, 'I am where I come from.'

'More tea, Dora?'

Yes, why not. I am where I come from. Netty refilling the kettle, putting it on the stove. Dora's stove, Dora's kettle, Dora's taps, plates, black dresser, floor, ceiling, table, sugar canister and kitchen sink.

'Morality's back with her mother then?'

'She liked town.'

'Ah, but home's home,' said Netty, 'When all's said.'

SIXTEEN

The powers of recovery are great. Imagine Dora's
body – open, laid out on the slab, internal organs
compressed, compacted, all hunched up. The heart
hasn't room to flutter, wouldn't risk a leap: Dora's
heart as hollow as the next man's, the main organ of
her circulatory system, doing what it was made to do,
contracting and relaxing, pumping round the blood.

In this semi-moribund emotional condition it is
amazing what can be achieved. What can be mooted
in the morning, discussed around an office desk that
same afternoon. For example, it is quite within the
bounds to discuss whether a woman who was probably the mother of your husband's child, should be
given one of the cottages or a room in your own
house. A room in your own house, imagine! How
solicitous one could be about something that broke
all the bones in your face with jealousy, that winded
you with hate. Maggie could move into Mrs Pierce's,
there she could be independent but not isolated. Close
to Netty but not under her busy, size-five feet. And
once this was decided it was easy to oversee the
preparations. Morality came up at the weekend and
she, Dora and the twins walked down to see what
needed to be done.

The house smelt of old frying, mice and damp bedding. Hairpins and spilt powder on the glass-topped dressing table, bits of used cotton wool, torn paper. Old tubes in the bathroom cabinet, white hair in the plug hole of the basin, dust and fluff in all the corners and beneath the bed. The children turned the mattresses in search of money, Morality found a florid bed jacket in the press, 'It's reversible Dora.'

'Good luck to it then.'

Satin, peach and powder blue.

Everything was damp. Age or Netty's fist had subdued the demented twin who behaved with admirable restraint pouring petrol on the bonfire. So cold you could see your breath in the house.

Dora and Morality. 'Don't let's bother with all that boring preparation.'

Slapping on white paint.

Loot from the house was shared unequally. Netty, who was already a beneficiary – she had inherited the sons and their appetites and pinched the clump of Mrs Pierce's favourite pinks 'for its own sake' while the body was still warm – was the first to take her pick. Mole fingers scrabbling through the kitchen cupboards, only taking, she insisted, what no one else would want. Dora didn't want anything and was hardly exuberant when Lydney presented her with Mrs P's old treadle sewing machine in perfect work-ing order. How come that she, who hated sewing, was haunted by these awful brutes?

'Maggie's going to need some curtains, Dora.'

'Well, I'm not going to do anything immediately.'

'In your own time,' he said.

And the peace, the under the eaves peace, came back again, as if it were the nature of the place.

'I detest sewing, each stitch is a nightmare,' she told Lydney as he leant over her to see what she was doing.

'You're cold. You'd be warmer in the kitchen.'

He hulked the old treadle in front of him, it hacked him on the shins.

'Light or heat. Make your choice.'

'Definitely heat.'

He set it at the far end of the kitchen near the stove.

As she threaded the cylindrical bobbin she swore if she thought anyone was listening, 'bloody awkward thing.' Moving to a window to thread it up. Netty handing the needle to Maggie, last year, out in the summer sunshine, 'Go on, your eyes are better than mine.'

Children's children, in bed with Stephen; I can't bear to think about you, I still love you, are you dead?

The curtains had to be cut down from longer, wider curtains; not just the curtains but the linings, which meant ripping the tape off the top and removing the curtain hooks and finding the discipline to put them safely somewhere in a jar. It meant measuring, cutting, ironing, measuring again and sewing. Four hems to each window, eight side seams, two lines of tape, replacing the curtain hooks . . . in this house with only one pair of scissors, blunt, middle-sized. Funny to work with Mrs Pierce's things, get absorbed in measuring and not thinking, making a cup of coffee to keep you going then treading on the chalk you meant to mark with, chalk dropped on the floor by the machine. The spice box for the buttons, I won't be wanting these surely? The toffee tin with its reels of cotton, sharps and big-eyed darning needles stuck into a book with leaves of faded lint.

There hadn't been a baby up at Carver for fifteen years; Morality had been the last. Somehow everyone had something; soap, a tin of talcum powder, a hat with a bobble and ear flaps, a wooden rattle with a silver bell, a hyacinth for a sunny window, wood chopped and stacked up under cover for the fire. A wedding was a wedding, a baby was a baby, cosy, cosy all the way, home's home.

Dora pulling faces in the kitchen, a new set of kittens playing with a reel of thread. Cursing as she unpicked a seam with her own nail scissors, Lydney coming in to put the kettle on. And she found that she'd make an excuse and go into the apple-scented scullery where he rolled his sleeves up to wash his arms, 'Touch me,' she begged him silently, 'someone hold me.' But if he chanced to brush against her she held herself away.

'Watch where you drop your ash, for God's sake Morality!'

'Sorry.'

'Just get out from under my feet if you're not going to do anything.'

'All right, I'm going.'

Her scullery, her cold corridors, her house. Alice's ghost now tangible, forbidding. Empty bottles right in there at the back of the airing cupboard, a place where a son would never look.

'Dora?'

'What?'

'I was just wondering . . .'

'What?'

'You know the menopause . . . ?'

'Not intimately, no.'

'I just wondered . . . ?'

'For God's sake, what?'

'You might be suffering from it. I mean you might be getting it. It might be making you . . .'

'What?'

'You never used to be so nasty.'

'I just like a bit of peace in my own house sometimes Morality!'

They gave her peace, the rock surrounded by the water, the silence deepened with each passing day.

SEVENTEEN

When she touched the baby she thought her heart would break. So small, Maggie carried it around on one of Netty's little stump work cushions. It was tiny and still a little mottled, blue-eyed. 'The blue will probably change,' said Netty, who knew everything. Blue-eyed and brown-haired beneath the bonnet with the bobble and the ear flaps. Tiny fingers one could stretch and look at, marvelling at the little knuckles and the perfect nails, while it lay still fast asleep. Maggie called it Girlay. It smelt beautiful, it felt silky.

'Not a mark on her,' Morality said as if she'd had some part in the production, 'perfect.'

The little arms, quite chubby already between the elbow and the wrist.

How did my mother bear it when my brother died? Why didn't I have one of these? Dora wanted to take it away and kiss it, kiss it, kiss it.

'She'll be spoilt rotten,' Maggie said enjoying the attention and, indeed, the baby was scarcely ever in its crib but spent its first winter of life going from lap to lap, shoulder to shoulder, cradled in everybody's arms.

'She looks contented.'

'She has every reason to be.'

Only squalling as Maggie changed its clothes so many times, as if it were a dolly, changing it all the time to keep it pretty.

Morality's done her mother's hair again, champagne blonde, apparently she's really looking good. Pam says she'll come up on one of her afternoons off if she can get a lift with someone but, 'You know, this and that.' She hasn't made it yet.

Tom Allen, on the other hand, can't keep himself away. Cycling across the hills to do his courting, his receding hair neatly combed, his forehead looking domelike. At first he came on Sundays for the company, pulling his chair up at Dora's, at the Freres, now he cycles straight to Maggie's, removing his bicycle clips, smoothing down those last wisps of hair.

Netty says she's seen it coming and is very much in two minds, as if the decision were up to her. Some fairly monumental things are now discussed around her kitchen table – always wiped of every crumb – and not a word is said until Enda has been fed and watered and sent off out of it, until the twins are fast asleep in bed:

Whether a man was better than no man, whether a man could take on the responsibility of someone else's child?

Maggie wasn't made to work, this seemed to be the nub of it.

A young girl like Maggie, plenty of time to add a few new faces at the table; she didn't want Girlay growing up on her own, now did she?

Tom . . . ? Hardly in the first flush of youth but

there were no men to be had and better a local man than some stranger; a stranger wouldn't do at all.

Maggie had a list of conditions. She wasn't looking for anybody, not with all the time with Girlay. Netty had words with her daughter, soon put her daughter straight.

'To see him with the baby, Maggie . . .' Well, a baby needed a father, and Tom could be trusted, he worked like a cart horse – so that was it – he was just like Enda, working like a cart horse, behaving like a sheep.

And privately, to others, Netty Frere talked of marriage bells for two. Maggie and Tom Allen and . . . well, stranger things have happened, Lydney and Dora? Tell me this, then? Why else would he put himself to such expense, oversee the rebuilding of the church?

Morality passed the gossip on to Dora.

'Sounds like the end of a pantomime,' Dora said.

The feast of the White Saint came and went again, meeting down at Hooley's Field by Stephen's little trees. Father Cuffe went through his mumbling act, no one could hear anything anyway for the flapping of the canvas on the church roof, the scaffolding around the building, like a skeleton outside the body's flesh.

Dora had an eye for one of the builders, everybody noticed that. The gaffer who'd had more women than hot dinners. Morality was quite impressed. He had lost a finger on his right hand and rumour had it that he didn't know where he'd left it. He had not at first singled Dora out from the little group because she had indeed become like them. They who became monosyllabic and sulky looking when faced with a foreigner, a member of the chorus dressed against the freezing weather in a shabby coat and hat.

The builders camped out in one of the cottages that Stephen had done up, everything happened over at The Sevens these days, at The Sevens there was life. Often there was the sound of singing in the evenings, Girlay passed from knee to knee and shoulder to shoulder. The gaffer was a born performer, he had confidence and pace. He could do anything with his hands, more ribaldry, cut out paper, do magic knots, make shadow pictures on the wall. Dora winced a bit when she heard these details from Morality. There was something about him, his self-containment, that attracted her; she could take or leave the shadow pictures and the magic knots.

'Could he replace the windows for her on the angel gallery?'

'Yes!'

The glass came up from Midway. It was a transformation. Dora hung about without much subtlety watching while he worked. He loved this room, he really admired the angel ceiling. To work on the church and now to be asked to work up here for her, he was enraptured by all of it, 'You know why, don't you?'

Dora played it coy.

He thought she might have guessed. Well, in his state he was sure it showed, he felt so changed by it, felt that it beamed right out of him . . .

'Tell me,' Dora so desperate for a leak to be sprung, for some relief. It seemed a crying shame. She beamed back bravely, 'Terrific.' Terrific to be told by him that he had decided to join the priesthood, to give himself to God.

God! Father Cuffe wasn't good enough, well that was understandable. God had to take the gaffer too. Christ. Dora sat up in her transformed room, hung out of the window listening to the carousing going on across the road.

Lydney came up behind her, 'I've been all over looking for you, Dora. I think I may have found a car.'

She did not put her arms around his neck or leap up in the air, perhaps she hadn't understood him.

'A car. For you.'

'I don't want a car.'

'Don't be like that, Dora. Everyone wants a car.'

She wanted something but it wasn't a bloody car! Dora closed the window and sat down on the chestnut chair. She expected an argument with Lydney, she rather looked forward to disappointing and annoying him, it gave her quite a lift. But he remained standing and something in his face persuaded her that he had no appetite for the fight. In fact, he was actually going to walk out on her! He got as far as the door before she called him back, 'What do you think of the windows?'

'Why won't you have the car?'

'Why don't we have some tea together? Sit down for a minute, I'll go and get a cup.'

He sat down in Stephen's chair, but he wasn't happy; she brought some tea for him.

'Now what about the car then?' he insisted.

That was more like it, but the sound of singing from across the road, how could God do this to her?

'Why would I need a car?'

'Don't have the car!' the man exploded. 'Don't have it. Forget it. Forget all about the car. Sit up here like a wailing woman, wait for Stephen, waste your life. Look in the mirror at the way your mouth turns down. Watch me out of the window and don't face up. Life is short, Dora, you have to grab what you can along the road. Do something for yourself before it's too late. He's not going to come walking back in.'

'I'll kill myself.'

'Strikes me you're already halfway there.'

'He'll come next month.'

'You know my position,' he said, for he was proposing to her in his own way. 'You just have to say the word.'

EIGHTEEN

Every day since the day Stephen had left she had imagined him returning. He would stand out from a group of men, she wouldn't distinguish him until he said her name. He would get off the bus at Midway, someone on the scaffolding would spy him walking up. A car would bring him, or a stranger would arrive with a message for her, that handwriting on a note. Suddenly, somewhere, he would be there behind her and would call her name. Something would happen to save her, she was only twenty-six.

Some days she woke up and she was sure that he was dead. These were the days when Alice's ghost seemed nearly tangible, dogged her lonely footsteps round the house. But other days were quite different, other days when everything seemed to point to his return. Some days, even now, she had a sense that he was near her, a feeling so strong that she would dash upstairs and wash her hair, change her dress, stand there shaking in front of the mirror with the cherub with the missing foot. She prayed, of course she did. Spoke to Stephen in prayers, that whatever he had or hadn't done, she would understand. That nothing mattered to her except simply having him come back. She read every article in the newspaper and lists of political prisoners now released drove her, if not yet to drink, then nearly to distraction. For there were stories in the paper, an amnesty for political prisoners arrested on suspicion, against whom nothing had been proved. Was Stephen one of these? Stories all the time these days of people coming back.

They were paid a sum of money and given a suitcase and a suit. Photos in the paper. Some of them had been in since the start of it, middle-aged men who might or might not be innocent, who had to learn to cope with peace. Walking back to a landscape different from that long remembered, to children who didn't know them or to children who had children of their own. To wives who had found someone else, to wives who'd swopped sides or collaborated, to wives whose imaginations differed. Junior back in lyrical mode, 'A clash of dreams'. Back to families who in some way or another had managed to live without them, 'Bitter Pills'. Work was found for them, money earned, a space in the bed . . . It was at this point that Dora became infuriated by what she was reading. She'd throw the paper to the floor.

Release had come too late for them, the story went. They missed the companionship of other prisoners. Falling over was it, now they were no longer shackled to the other men? The narcotic anticipation of freedom meant that freedom was an anti-climax after all. Poor lambs. They had gone in the thick and excitement of action and returned to stagnation, stillness and a compromise which they found dispiriting. They were out of step. They cherished solitude. 'Walking Wounded' well she could cope with that. Wounded yes, but not like her brother, wounded but able to toddle about a bit. Wounded, well she felt pretty rough herself! She didn't have to look into the mirror, she knew that something had atrophied, shrivelled up. That absence we recognise in one another but never mention; so who isn't wounded? So what's new? She saw it in her own face and, surprisingly, beneath the champagne blonde hair, in Pam's.

She imagined Stephen hitching along the road they had cycled. They should have made love by that empty house: 'You have to grab what you can along the road.'

Tea at Netty's was at six, you could smell the frying from across the road. Maggie had gone down to Pam's at Midway for the evening, gave Dora the baby and a bottle, 'just in case'. She had the baby and nursed it, an April evening after a rainstorm; the sky looked pale and fragile as if it were holding out, but only just, against the coming night. She'd got the windows now, the front of the house was reborn again although the new glass could not be like the old. Flakes of old dry paint which called for some domestic reaction, and the lovely linseed smell of putty.

He would come upstairs and call her Dora.

Netty shouting 'Tea!' set up a barking from the dogs. Staring through the new glass watching the darkness coming, this year, last year, time immemorial, someone help me please!

The road dusty in the summer, sodden in the autumn, the road made artificially green for the winter wedding, the road that renews itself each spring. Inside us all there is a green road to the heart. Looking through the new glass of the window at the shut of the day. Come on Dora, jump!

She loved this baby as she had loved Stephen, a long time ago. She loved the inside of her elbows, the soft down on her cheeks and back, her fingers, her eyes, still blue, keeping her gaze. She loved her, she loved her, and when she touched her something fluttered into life within her. it hurt like hell, like real pins and needles, it hurt her as the cone began to reopen and the love came flooding back into her hand.

Now she snuggled the baby up on the chestnut chair, wedging her in with a cushion so she couldn't fall. She went to the window, the baby lay under the ceiling – angels guard your couch. Morality was practising reversing in the yard, she heard the crunch and the 'Effin B!' after it as the bumper hit the wall.

CODA

The bus drops me off on the Sky Road, I cross over and it's still turning its nose into the lay-by and grunting. I've seen it so many times: the driver spinning the steering wheel, reversing, edging forwards, sometimes he gets out, his urine steaming on the road. I raise my hand to him, I'm lucky if I get a nod of the head. He buttons up his trousers in a hurry, he isn't happy about coming out this far. I'm stiff from that old bus, the plastic seats mended by the bus company, torn again by so many children, initials, love hearts, swear words. I know all its squeaks and groans, and especially how cold it is, the feel of the aluminium bar as I get on and off. I know every inch of the switchback road that comes from the town on the great lakes; an hour's journey. I could probably do the swings back and forth – how you have to tense this bit then that bit of your body not to slide right off the seat – quite automatically. The driver loves it too, swinging into those long curves. I suppose I am the same age as the driver now. In dreams I am an adult and I travel on my own.

I climb upwards and I can see the bus for a long time. I cross Gobbins to Carver; Starveall is the only house on the other side and its smoke can be seen from where I am. I go up Carver Hill where the metalled road is entirely broken up by the water that comes down, finding its own level in the winter. I hop across these rivulets, sometimes bits of furze bush all washed down. I put distance between myself and water and yet here the water sometimes makes a river in the road.

I cross the yard, dirty snow and straw, and in through the side door where the brick floor is indented from years and years of boots. The doors are all latches. I know the sound of every little click; through the sculleries each with its own distinctive smell, into the kitchen. The kitchen, always a mess, is broken up now, the cupboard doors are off, the drawer hangs out of the black dresser and I pick my way across the floor, things rolling, yet the top is still on the sugar canister. I put the kettle on for tea and then open the oven door of the stove to warm my back and just look simply at the long and blank and empty kitchen table. There's still never a teaspoon and I wash one up under the cold tap. I think it's got egg on it, and lift the egg off with my nail. Then I cover my tea with a sideplate, the passageways from the kitchen are always arctic, and go upstairs; silence, just the tinkle of the china plate and cup. I sit beneath a ceiling of angels, I keep the sideplate on the cup until I'm ready and sit there in my greatcoat drinking. I put my hand in my pocket and my hand is full of bits of green leaf, brittle and to be handled carefully lest it disintegrates altogether. I have to think about it carefully too; I feel it in my cold hands but I don't look at it. That's my dream, me, sitting in the room looking out and drinking tea in the greatcoat I got married in.